Table of Contents

BETWEEN YESTERDAY AND TOMORROW

Where Imagination and Reality Collide

By

Regina Arnold

INTRODUCTION

Welcome, dear reader, to a realm of raw emotions, revolutionary moments, and captivating stories.

Between Yesterday and Tomorrow - Where Imagination and Reality Collide is more than just a collection of creative tales. It's a composition of human experiences that resonate with the deepest corners of the soul.

With every turn of the page, you'll encounter characters who have weathered life's storms, love that defies time, and lessons that echo through the ages.

So, grab your favorite beverage, find your most comfortable spot, and let these stories carry you to a world where yesterday and tomorrow converge into today.

Happy reading!

WHAT DOES IT MEAN?

In the vast expanse of time and space,
      What's the meaning of this human race?
      A question that's pondered through the years,
      By thinkers, poets, and those with fears.
      Is it to love, to create, to learn,
      To leave a legacy when we are gone?
      Is it to find purpose, seek and grow,
      Or to simply live and let everything flow?
      Is it to find the joy in every breath,
      Or perhaps transcend our mortal death?
      Is it to make a difference, great or small,
      To enjoy life's pleasures, one and all?
      Perhaps the meaning lies in our own hearts,
      The secrets we uncover, one by one,
      A journey unique until we're done,
      A quest for truth, the reason we've begun.
      In the end, the meaning may not be found,
      But in the search, we find the joy profound,
      For in this world, there's beauty and light.
      What's true for you? Your meaning of life?

AULD LANG SYNE

Tim looked at the report on his weather app just to make sure they wouldn't have frozen noses, fingers, and toes by the time the clock struck midnight in Times Square.

He had those kooky, flashing glasses that everyone would be wearing laid out on the entry hall table so he wouldn't forget to take them. He had even pulled out an extra wool scarf and some ear warmers for Amanda because he knew how much she hated being cold. Watching him, Amanda smiled, trying to feel as excited as he obviously was. But she just couldn't muster it.

He'd been trying his best for the past year to lift her spirits after she lost a member of her Happy Trails Gals tribe. Carrie had gone in for a routine surgery that should have been successful, but something went terribly wrong and she wasn't healing like the surgeon expected. Her major organs failed and she passed away suddenly a year ago on New Year's Eve.

The remaining members of the tribe were shocked and heartbroken. A gaping hole was left in four hearts that night. One that could never be filled by another human being.

They all lived in different cities, spread out across the country, but each year they would take an adventure together, meeting up somewhere for a much-needed reunion.

Carrie was in the final stage of an obnoxious divorce, currently retiring from her job at the postal service, and finally going to be able to get out on her own, buying a house for herself for the first time in her 62 years. Talk about an adventure!

She was thrilled and looking forward with great anticipation to her new life, and putting a controlling husband behind her. When the Happy Trails tribe had gathered the previous September on the west coast for their annual get-together, they all toasted her freedom with a little too much champagne. They spent most of the night talking and laughing around a huge bonfire like teenage girls with their lives ahead of them.

Carrie stopped, held up her hand and, with tears welling up in her eyes, raised her champagne flute and said in her magnetic southern drawl, "I love y'all so much and don't know what my life would be without you in it. You've been my strongest supporters and encouraged me when I was scared as hell to take this leap. Cheers and happy trails, my lovelies."

Amanda was replaying Carrie's bonfire conversation in her head when Tim said, "It's gonna be so much fun watching the ball drop in Times Square this year, don't you think, babe? I've wanted to be there in person since I first saw it on mom and dad's old TV."

Amanda didn't want to hurt him or dampen his enthusiasm. He was such a good guy. The best she'd ever known. Their marriage had hit the skids on occasion, but they managed to work through their differences with the help of counseling. At times, she wondered how someone with his calm demeanor could put up with her free-for-all personality. Even during the rough times, he would manage to share his thoughts about their issues in a patient, rational manner. "I guess everybody with a gypsy soul needs a true north," she thought. Tim was hers.

But, on the other hand, many times she wished he would just blow up and get it all out on the table, because her intuition told her that there was something simmering just under the surface.

"Tim, I know you're really looking forward to this and I'd love to have as much enthusiasm about it as you, but I'm not feeling it. The masses of people, the chaos, the noise ... I just can't, sweetheart. You go ahead and have a blast tonight. Just one thing. Please be careful. I know there will be a huge police presence and security, but keep your eyes and ears open. There's a good chance someone will use this event to make some sort of political statement, if you know what I mean."

"No, babe. I'm not going without you. No freakin' way. But for your sake, can't you tuck your sadness away just for tonight? Are you gonna stop your life every New Year's Eve because of Carrie? You know she wouldn't want that. She loved to have fun and you always have, too."

The distressed look in his eyes made her cringe with self-reproach, which wasn't like her at all ... until now. As much as she loved him, it was time to own her feelings and her grief. There had been too much pain over the years with their marital issues, her own mother's passing, and now it seemed like Carrie's death was bringing it all to the surface. No more stuffing her emotions for the sake of anyone else. It wasn't healthy and she knew it.

"Listen, honey. Please hear me. I'm not going, and there's no point in you trying to convince me otherwise. Believe me,

I'll be fine right here with Dutch, a bowl of popcorn and some bubbly."

Dutch was their Golden Retriever, who, sound asleep at her feet right then, was Amanda's sidekick and went almost everywhere with her. Tim often teased her that their dog loved her more than him.

He could see that no matter what he said or how gently he asked, it was a lost cause. "OK, fine. Let her sit here in her misery," he thought, but didn't say it out loud. He stared at her for a minute with a pang of bitterness, then picked up the silly glasses, his coat and gloves and walked out the door without looking back.

That's when the epiphany hit her hard – grief doesn't have any rules, someone else's timetable, or a GPS. It comes in waves, and like the ones on the west coast, no two hold the same force. Each wave of grief is unique, carrying with it a mix of emotions that can be as unpredictable as the tides. But as she learned to navigate these turbulent waters, she found comfort in the understanding that her journey was her own, and that healing would come in its own time.

GODDESS OF THE EMBERS

On the night Pyra was born, as the clock in the square chimed midnight, a tempestuous storm shrouded the waxing Gibbous moon. As thunder and lightning awakened the slumbering village, secrets were being whispered to the newborn's soul. Her grandmother, the midwife, sensing the extraordinary essence of this special child, knew that Pyra was destined to illuminate the world with remarkable gifts.

Yet, as Pyra grew into womanhood, her prophetic visions only brought her ridicule and scorn from her peers, the very people she sought to enlighten. Crushed by their cruelty, Pyra's radiance began to fade, and she withdrew into the shadows. But her grandmother's words of inspiration always lingered in her memory, urging her to reclaim her light. It was during those darkest moments that Pyra sought solace in the mystical forest, where her lonely heart felt safe.

Now, in the loving embrace of nature, where ancient trees shared their energy with the wind, Pyra, the Goddess of Fire, stirred from her slumber. As the last rays of sunlight faded, she arose, her fiery locks blazing with an inner light. With a gentle touch of her fingertips, she ignited a bonfire, and the flames responded to her presence, dancing in rhythmic harmony.

Pyra's hair, a wild tangle of gold and copper, was adorned with stars - tiny, twinkling celestial fragments that shimmered like diamonds. As she moved, the stars swirled around her, weaving a cosmic melody that synchronized with the crackling flames. The air was filled with the sweet aroma of burning wood and the promise of transformation.

Her ethereal robe, with hues of emerald green and aquamarine blue, undulated like a lover's caress as she glided across the forest floor, its delicate folds whispering secrets to the trees, enticing them to surrender to the enchantment of her graceful waltz.

With each step, Pyra's power grew, and the bonfire responded, its flames leaping higher, as if reaching for the heavens. Her dance was a primal summoning, calling forth the ancient magic that coursed through her veins. The stars in her hair pulsed with an otherworldly energy, filling the night air with electricity. As her dance reached its climax, the forest came alive. Trees swayed in unison to the rhythm, their branches whispering even more secrets to the wind. Creatures of the night – fireflies, owls, and wolves – gathered at the perimeter, mesmerized by the spectacle. The Goddess's dance was a symphony of light, sound, and primal energy, woven together in unconditional love.

The night wind responded to her call, stirring the forest's sleeping soul. The air was filled with the heady aroma of pine, its crisp scent of resin, bringing the ancient knowledge of the trees to life. The earthy fragrance of Mother Earth herself rose from the forest floor, a rich, loamy smell that spoke of fertility and rebirth. Seeping through these primal scents was the promise of a soft rain, its gentle patter whispering its own secrets to the forest, bringing hope and renewal to the land. The wind carried the rich blend of aromas on its gentle currents, enveloping Pyra, nourishing her spirit with every breath and awakening the deep magic that had always been inside her.

Never again would she question her gift, for in this moment, Pyra knew that her power was not a curse, but a sacred blessing. The flames that danced at her fingertips, the stars that twinkled in her hair, and the whispers of the forest all converged to confirm her true nature. The doubts that had once plagued her, the fears that had made her hide her light, were silenced by the radiant confidence that now burned once again in her soul. Pyra's gift was a part of her, a manifestation of her deepest essence, and she vowed to nurture it, to let it shine brightly for all to see.

The Goddess of Fire, once timid and uncertain, now stood tall, her heart encouraged by her grandmother's words and an unshakeable faith in living her soul's true purpose.

LUCY'S CHALLENGE

Lucy could sense the end was getting closer, feeling it in strange new ways. It was only Doug who didn't. The date had been chosen and all the arrangements meticulously made.

It was time. He was on his way and would be there any minute. She choked back the lump in her throat as she briskly wiped her eyes, a thousand jumbled thoughts racing through her head. Was she handling this right? For his sake and not hers?

When she opened the heavy oak front door, the pained look on her face was only softened by the amber glow from a fading sun. Doug could tell something was up. She had been a little off lately and each time he asked her what was wrong, she would smile and assure him that everything was fine. Lucy, being Lucy, would then promptly change the subject.

She had gotten so good at it that she wondered if there was some unseen force speaking through her physical body, preparing her, providing the fortitude that she would need to pull this off. The only thing that made her fearful was knowing that, after today, she would never be held in his loving arms again.

He had the picnic basket stocked with a bottle of Merlot, a fresh loaf of her favorite crusty bread, Greek olives and Havarti cheese. He knew her so well.

"Shall we go, my love?" he asked. "The sun's hugging the horizon and if we're going to make it to the beach in time to see it go down, we should get a move on."

So many times during the last three months she had wanted to burst into tears, to release the sorrow, and tell him everything. But her devoted love for him stopped her each time until it got a little easier to hold it in. Right now, though, a feeling of panic creeped in as she heard him say those words 'my love,' knowing it would be the last time she would hear them.

At last they were alone together in their intimate little cove on the beach, the last warm rays of the sun streaming across their faces. He was about to kiss her when she looked at him and said, "I have a challenge for you, my darling. I want to see if you can live a whole day, 24 hours, without me. No communication. No texts. No phone calls. No visits. If you can do it, I'll love you forever."

Shocked, he snapped his head back and started to protest but she placed her fingers over his lips and whispered, "Promise me. Please."

Doug kept his promise. But when the 24 hours had passed, he raced excitedly to her house only to find her parents, tears falling in stunned silence. Her mother handed him the small envelope.

Hands trembling, he read the note, "You did it, baby. Now please do it every day. I'll love you and watch over you forever."

When the oncologist had told Lucy it was time to get her affairs in order, she knew that her decision, while excruciating, was necessary to protect her loved ones from the unbearable pain of watching her brain and body deteriorate.

Lucy swallowed the medication she'd been saving up, hoping for a peaceful end. She closed her eyes, her final thoughts drifting to Doug and her parents, praying that they would, one day, find solace in the joyful memories of their time together.

DRAGONSLAYER

In the kingdom of Eldrid, Sir Cedric, the most noble of all the knights, was known for his bravery and unwavering loyalty to the crown. His chiseled features and piercing blue eyes made him a favorite among the ladies, but his heart belonged entirely to his kingdom and the people he swore to protect.

One day when the air was heavy with dark clouds gathering over the land, news of a ferocious dragon spread like wildfire. An unknown force had awakened the beast from its slumber and was now terrorizing the countryside, setting fire to the villages and devouring livestock. The king, desperate to save his people, summoned Sir Cedric to face the monstrous creature.

Upon his return from surveying the dragon's cave, Cedric addressed the king, "Your Majesty, I have returned from the dragon's lair, and I regret to inform you that the beast remains a threat to our kingdom."

"Sir Cedric, your bravery is unmatched, and I have faith in your ability to stop the dragon's destruction. What do you require to complete this mission?

"I believe a team of skilled knights, well-equipped with weapons and armor, could help us face the dragon together. Additionally, I would seek the counsel of our wisest sages to learn more about the creature's weaknesses.

"Very well, Cedric. I shall call the inhabitants of Eldrid to gather in prayer, assemble a team of our finest knights, and consult our scholars to aid you in your quest. We must do everything in our power to protect our kingdom from this mighty threat.

"Thank you, Your Majesty. With your support and the strength of our kingdom behind us, we shall vanquish the dragon and restore peace once again to Eldrid."

With sharpened swords in hand and shields at the ready, Sir Cedric and his band of intrepid knights ventured deep into the dragon's lair, navigating treacherous caverns and dodging deadly booby traps. The air grew thick with the stench of sulfur, and the ground trembled beneath their feet as the dragon's thunderous roar echoed through the tunnels.

With Sir Cedric leading the charge, he rounded a corner and came face to face with evil incarnate – the colossal beast. Its scales glistened like polished obsidian, and its eyes burned with a demon-like red fire. Without hesitation and a prayer on his lips, the knight steeled his nerves and charged forward, his sword slashing through the air with deadly precision.

In a battle that would be spoken of for generations, Sir Cedric and the dragon clashed in a fierce barrage of steel and flames. The band of brothers, closing in from behind, saw that the knight's skill and determination were matched only by the dragon's raw power and cunning. It seemed as though time stood still, neither combatant willing to yield. Cedric shouted to his knights to stand back, knowing that one swipe from the dragon's front claws would take them all down.

Yet, as the sun dipped below the horizon and darkness enveloped the land, a glimmer of hope shone in Cedric's heart.

He saw a weakness in the dragon's defenses, a chink in its seemingly impenetrable armor. With all his strength and a mighty roar of his own, the knight lunged forward and rammed his sword strategically into the center of the demon's chest, ending its reign of terror once and for all. The dragon's last deadly gasp was heard throughout the entire kingdom.

As Sir Cedric emerged from the lair, his armor battered and his body bruised, he was greeted by the cheers of his grateful people. The kingdom of Eldrid was at peace once more, thanks to the heroism of their beloved knight.

Sir Cedric's legend would live on for centuries, a testament to the power of prayer, courage, and the unwavering spirit of a true hero who defeated evil.

MEGAN'S ESCAPE

It was an unusually cold, snowy March in northeastern Iowa that year, three months before James would graduate from high school.

12-year old Megan asked her brother, "Do you like him?" 17-year old James replied, "No, but Mom does. Do *you* like him?"

"No. He scares me."

And so it began. Her life of being cherished by her mother, brother, and grandparents would turn into an inescapable fear that would surround her for six more years before she could leave home. James would escape right after his graduation.

When their father, Norman, divorced their mother, Catherine, Megan was just four years old; James was already nine. Although Megan had no memories of living with their father, James did, and he would happily share these recollections with her whenever she asked.

Norman was a gentle man, soft-spoken, kind and compassionate. Their soon-to-be stepfather, Lee, was just the opposite, always grumbling about something. He had a good job as an electrical engineer, wearing a suit and tie to work every day and those ugly wingtip shoes. The very shoes that Megan would soon dread the sound of each evening when he came through the door.

Catherine and Lee's wedding took place on a weekend in May when Megan and James were visiting their grandparents, 135 miles away. They weren't invited and didn't even know it was happening. It was all planned that way. Years later Megan would realize the impact of their hush-hush nuptials.

Shortly after Catherine and Lee came home, they told the kids they were married and he was being transferred to San Francisco. They would all be leaving the day after James graduated. Stunned and angry, James looked at them both, yelled that he wasn't going with them and bolted out of the house. Megan would never forget the pained look on his face as he glanced over his shoulder at her.

Catherine ran after him but he had already pulled away from the curb, peeling out in his old black Chevy Bel Air. Megan's fear intensified. What if he really didn't go with them? Even though they fought sometimes, as siblings naturally do, her big brother was her protector.

Graduation day came in early June and the whole family was there, including their dad's sister, Aunt Gayle. But no dad. They would find out later from Aunt Gayle that he wanted to come, but Catherine told him he wasn't welcome. They would also find out, as they grew older, about the many times he wanted to take James and Megan for a weekend and Catherine refused. Years later, Norman still held on to the pictures that Gayle took at James' graduation. For Norman, many battles were fought and lost in secret.

James ended up staying in Iowa with Catherine's brother so that he could start college while Catherine, Lee, and Megan moved to California. It was a long drive, and Megan cried silent tears the whole way. Tears of sadness at leaving the cocoon of her life in Iowa, around her friends and family who loved her, and tears of rage at how she was yanked away with no say in the matter.

Her Grandpa had become her champion, the one who let her play in his workshop all day when she wanted to. He'd give her and her friends nickels to buy sodas at the corner market. Then she would go in the house and see what Grandma was doing. Grandma, the nurturer, would walk with her to the ice cream parlor and buy her a double scoop of her favorite black walnut ice cream.

And the hot, muggy summer nights on the porch swing with Grandpa, listening to his stories, his wisdom seeping into her young bones, hearing the chains creak on the swing as it swayed back and forth, like a soothing lullaby. Every night Megan would tease Grandpa that he forgot to oil the chains and every night they would both chuckle about it. She was prone to getting welts when summer mosquitoes started biting, so Grandpa screened in the front porch for her protection. Those memories would comfort her in times to come.

Once settled in San Francisco, Catherine enrolled Megan in an all girl Catholic school. She didn't want her to be in one of those jumbo public schools, so that was the only other option.

Megan hated the city bus ride to and from school, the oppressive style of the nuns' teaching, having to make new friends, wearing a scratchy wool uniform every day, not being able to talk in the halls, and unseen eyes watching the girls' every move. She immersed herself into learning, but it was still a shock to her entire being after living in a small town in Iowa where everybody knew everybody. Here she knew no one.

Later, when she did make some friends, she was afraid to invite them to sleep over at her house because of Lee, always angry and grumbling about something, especially after he'd had a couple of drinks to 'unwind.' If they made too much noise, he got mad. If they went outside to play yard darts, he got mad, telling them they were disturbing the neighbors. On many nights after she went to bed, she would hear Catherine and Lee fighting, which always escalated into her mom screaming at him. She quickly learned how to walk on eggshells and stopped inviting her friends over at all.

Megan eventually became close friends with three other girls, all of whom had normal families with brothers and sisters who became like siblings to her. One in particular, Vicki, was always inviting her to have dinner and spend the night. Vicki's parents were loving, gentle people and she cherished her time with them.

There was laughter and playfulness around their dinner table. She learned how to play poker, dominos, Monopoly, and do crafts with the girls. The boys were always teasing them, including Megan, much like James used to do. Especially when they were learning how to apply makeup for the first time and emerged from Vi's room resembling circus clowns.

When James came to San Francisco for a visit, everything was going fine until Lee came home drunk one night and started badgering him about not moving to California with them, telling him it broke Catherine's heart. It escalated to the point of Lee pulling his fist back, ready to strike James in the face.

Megan screamed for him to stop as Catherine came running into the room and grabbed him by the shirt collar just before he hit James. One thing led to another. Catherine ran to the kitchen and came back with a knife, threatening Lee that if he didn't leave, she would kill him. It all happened so fast. He stormed out, not coming home until the next morning, reeking of stale beer and cigarettes. Another night of shrinking and no sleep for Megan.

James left the next day to go back to Iowa. Megan sobbed and begged him to take her with him. He wanted to, but Catherine wouldn't have it. He told Megan years later that he regretted not putting her in the car with him that day and speeding away. Two hearts broken once more.

Megan met Darren the summer before her senior year of high school. The night she graduated at 17, he put an engagement ring on her finger and told her as soon as she turned 18, they would be married.

Three months after her 18th birthday, they eloped to Lake Tahoe and were married by a justice of the peace. She thought she loved him. But what she really loved was the escape.

PICKING UP THE PIECES

It wasn't long after the sudden death of her son, Ryan, that Sheila discovered her lover's secret – infidelity. Her world shattered like delicate crystal. The pain from losing Ryan was suffocating, but this discovery only added to the heavy weight that crushed her heart. She felt like she was drowning in a sea of despair, with no one throwing her a life preserver. Her constant question was why??

In the aftermath of Don's betrayal, Sheila's friends and family urged her to seek revenge, to expose and lash out at the one who had wronged her. But she knew the path of revenge would only lead to more suffering. Instead, she chose to go on a journey within, to confront the darkest corners of her own mind.

Not revealing where she was going, Sheila packed up what she would need and retreated to a secluded cabin at Mirror Lake, surrounded by the silence and majesty of the Ponderosa pines. She spent her days walking among the trees in silence, sitting by the lake, meditating, journaling, and exploring the maze of her inner self. She delved into the shadows, confronting the parts of herself she had long neglected and kept hidden from the world.

As she examined the depths of her own subconscious, she began to unravel the tangled threads of her past. She discovered the roots of her people-pleasing tendencies, as well as the loneliness from her childhood of being compared to her siblings. She finally came to grips with the need for validation that she never got from her narcissistic mother, and her fear of abandonment. It was then that she finally faced the aspects of herself that had attracted Don's betrayal in the first place, asking herself, "What part did I play in this?"

Coupled with the grief of losing her son, and beating herself up for making poor decisions, the process was ugly at times. There were sleepless nights and long days when the pain and anger threatened to consume her. But Sheila persevered, fueled by a burning desire to discover her sense of balance and reconstruct her life.

One night, after spending a tearful afternoon releasing her pain, she knew it was time to write a letter to Don, knowing she would never mail it. They hadn't spoken in over two years; she didn't even know where he was and didn't care.

Dear Don,

That day when I told you that I couldn't go on in this relationship, please know that I didn't make that decision lightly or to hurt you.

I understood you being upset and you told me you didn't want to talk about it then. I understood that, too. But as the days passed before you left, I was disappointed that you didn't ask, "What can we do to make this better?" I believe our break-up triggered memories of your past break-ups and how you ran from them, and maybe that made you feel vulnerable. But only you know if that's true or not.

After Ryan died, I tucked my grief into an invisible box, and tried to lock it away. I felt that if I grieved publicly, you wouldn't know how to deal with the discomfort it would bring for both of us. Knowing what I know now, that was a huge mistake on my part. Instead of silencing my screams, I should have vocalized my pain.

I asked if you ever went online to research what it's like for a mother to lose her child, or to get ideas about how to emotionally support her. You admitted that you hadn't, which made me feel like I never existed.

But let me go back to the beginning of our relationship for a minute. You moving in with me served a purpose, even though in hindsight, we both know it was too soon for you after your break-up with your wife and too soon for me after my husband's death. We weren't ready. Both of us needed more time for healing and self-reflection. It's so clear to me now and I feel like we are both responsible for not acknowledging it at the time.

Yes, we got to experience the chase, the infatuation, and future plans; got to know more about each other – our values, similar likes & dislikes; the fun travels we had together, as well as other things. Those were good times and happy memories.

But when I began to notice you pulling away, becoming distant, it became crystal clear that I was pouring my love and energy into our relationship and not getting anything back. It drained me dry. I tried to talk to you about it but you just shined it on like I was crazy.

All I wanted was stability, honest communication, loyalty, respect, and committed love. Not too much to ask because that's what makes a healthy relationship, and I feel like I gave all of that to you. I loved you and trusted you, Don.

We both said in the beginning that we wouldn't settle for less in relationships and that's still true for me, so maybe that phrase *about 'two souls who are destined to come together but not stay together' applies to us.*

I'm taking my time to learn about who I am now and know that I have to make my needs and desires a priority after a lifetime of putting other people first. This is not my ego; it's listening to my intuition ... those messages from my soul that I've been ignoring. I'm finally getting out of my own way to allow God to do his work for the highest good of all concerned.

I sincerely wish you well and hope you'll always have what you want and need. Do what makes you feel alive, Don. I am.

Sheila tore the letter into little pieces, placed them in a steel pot, and set them on fire, sending this chapter of her life up in smoke.

As she integrated the fragmented parts of her psyche, she began to feel a sense of wholeness, of unity. She started to see the world from a higher perspective, with fresh eyes, to appreciate the beauty and wonder that had been hidden beneath the surface of her logical mind. She had dug out the old long-buried childhood wounds that needed to be healed.

One morning, as she walked beside the lake in silence, Sheila felt the weight of her sorrow beginning to lift like the morning mist evaporating in the sun. She heard Ryan's voice echoing in her mind, "You're going to be OK, Mom." With tears of joy in her eyes, she knew that she was not the same woman who had been left behind. After evaluating all of her past and current relationships, she was stronger, wiser, and more compassionate about her choices.

Sheila returned to her life, but not to the same, worn-out patterns and relationships. She emerged like a butterfly from a cocoon, reborn and confident. Her eyes sparkled with a newfound sense of purpose, her heart filled with a deep desire to continue learning about self-awareness..

In the end, she understood that Don's betrayal was a blessing in disguise and that everything serves a purpose. It forced her to confront her shadows, work through her grief with radical acceptance, seek the truth within to make better choices in the future, and to reclaim her destiny – that of the strong woman who had lived under the surface her entire life.

HIGH TIDE CLYDE

Upon the vast and endless sea,
Sailed Captain Clyde, a heart so free.
His life was ruled by tide and gale,
His destiny, to endlessly sail.
Storms and tempests, he did brave,
His ship, his constant resting place.
The sea and its depths, his only home,
His heart, forevermore to roam.
But fate, in all her magical ways,
Had other plans for him to face.
A mighty storm, it did unfold,
A chance encounter, love untold.
A maiden fair, her ship did sink,
Her fate, a watery grave in the drink.
He saved her life, a bond was formed,
Their love, a gale, fiercely warmed.
No longer ruled by sea's embrace,
His heart, now bound to human grace.
Together, they sailed life's abundant sea,
A love, a force, to forever be.
So let us toast the captain bold,
Who found his heart, his love untold.
Their story, a testament of fate,

Of love that found a perfect mate.

THE MASKS WE WEAR

Pierre spent his days hiding behind a carefully crafted mask. It wasn't a visible mask made of fabric or metal, but of the lies and half-truths he told himself and others. As a child, he had endured unspeakable traumas that left deep wounds embedded in his soul. He was terrified to confront them, fearing they would consume him if he dared to acknowledge their presence.

As he grew older, Pierre's fear of vulnerability intensified. He built walls around his heart, ensuring that no one could ever get close enough to see the pain he carried. To the world, Pierre portrayed self-assurance, sometimes to the point of being cocky. Yet privately, he moped around in a self-imposed confinement, fearing change, and weighed down by his own memories.

When he met an intuitive woman named Lily, it didn't take her long to see through his carefully constructed mask. At first, he was petrified by her ability to observe the real him, but as time passed, he found himself drawn to her warmth and kindness. For the first time in his life, Pierre began to consider the possibility of confronting his childhood traumas and learning to trust in the power of vulnerability. There was a persistent nagging inside of him that wouldn't let go, but still he kept trying to silence it.

One evening as Lily and Pierre sat cuddled before a blazing fire, he noticed how quiet she had become.

"Is something bothering you, sweetheart?" he asked.

"I'm just having a hard time understanding why you're not being honest with me. I believed we were developing a deeper connection, but when I asked about your relationship with your parents, you suddenly shut down and shifted the conversation. Is there something you don't want to talk about?"

Pierre stiffened and retorted, "Nothing you can help with. You're not a psychologist, are you?"

For Lily, his question was a slap in the face. All she wanted to do was love and care for him, but his guardedness was making it impossible.

Despite his growing feelings for her, Pierre found himself unable to remove his mask. He felt like a tiger in a cage, unable to escape. As the days turned into weeks, and the weeks into months, his apprehension of being vulnerable continued to grow, driving a wedge between him and the woman he loved. Lily wanted to be patient, trying her best to make sense of Pierre's behavior, but realized that their relationship had deteriorated into one of merely tolerance, not trust and confidence. That's when she knew it had to end.

On her way to work one morning, she pulled up in front of Pierre's place, took a deep breath and knocked on the door. When he answered, she spoke her words carefully, but with confidence. "Pierre, this isn't working for either of us. I know you're not happy and neither am I. Let's just agree that it's time to stop pouring energy into something that isn't fulfilling. I'll always love you, but I can't be with you." She turned and walked away.

Pierre's inability to confront his past and embrace vulnerability had just cost him the one person who truly saw him for who he was. As he watched Lily walk away, he suddenly realized that the mask he wore to protect himself had only succeeded in driving away the love he so desperately craved. With a heavy heart, he pledged to confront his anxieties and shed the veil that had come to represent his anguish.

In the months that followed, Pierre found the courage to face his past and the traumas that had shaped him. After searching and locating a trusted therapist, he began the long, arduous process of healing. Together, they uncovered his fears and approached the source of his years of suffering.

With each passing day, Pierre felt his heart grow lighter, his spirit more free. He knew that he could never undo the past or reclaim the love he had lost, but he also understood that he was no longer the same man who had driven Lily away. He was stronger, braver, and more determined than ever to live a life unburdened by the weight of his past.

One day, 18 months later, as he walked through the park, he caught sight of a woman sitting on a bench. Her face was familiar, yet different somehow. As he approached her, his heart pounding in his chest, he realized who it was – Lily.

For a moment, they just stared at each other, the weight of their shared history heavy in the air between them. Then, with a tentative smile, Pierre reached out and took Lily's hand. As their fingers intertwined, he felt a warmth spread through his chest, a feeling of connection and understanding that transcended words. Together, they walked through the park, talking about their lives and the changes they had undergone since the day she left.

As the sun began to set, casting a warm glow over the park, Pierre knew that he had found the strength to embrace vulnerability and the courage to love without reservation.

Ultimately, it was his decision to come out from behind the mask and face his fears that allowed him to find true happiness and the love of the one woman he had always longed for.

TARGETED

Alicia Boukamp looked down at her gray boots, trying to stomp off the snow. At least her coat was reasonably dry. She hoped to remain obscure as she entered the crowded lobby of the Edgewater Hotel.

That's when she noticed the man with the scruffy salt and pepper beard in a worn out brown leather jacket following a few strides behind her. At first she thought he was merely someone trying to get in out of the frigid air, but normally people dressed like him didn't hang out in swanky hotel lobbies.

She had seen him lurking around her office building over the past few days, but never noticed him following her until now. Was it him who sent her the text to meet him here?

Then she saw the other man, standing over in the corner in a tattered, green military fatigue jacket, also looking out of place and trying to pretend he wasn't watching her. A surge of adrenaline hit as she prepared to turn and run. That's when she felt a hand grip her shoulder from behind.

"Stay calm, Alicia."

"How...?"

"How do I know your name? I'm supposed to. I'm here to help. You're a target," he whispered. "Don't turn around. Look straight ahead and start walking at a normal pace toward the elevators."

Alicia wasn't the kind of woman who frightened easily. She had already taken down one coffee plantation in South America engaged in child slave labor aimed at her country's population. Being a target wasn't new to her, but this felt different, more deadly. Her heart racing, she felt an overwhelming urge to flee, but to where?

He motioned her toward the elevator. "Pick up the pace now. Move your ass quick," he growled. She didn't waste any time doing what he told her and felt him close behind, shielding her, as they hustled toward the waiting elevator. A strange looking woman whom she had never seen before was there waiting, holding the doors open. As the doors were within an inch of closing, she caught a glimpse of the brown leather jacket.

Damn. That was close, but now she was able to exhale and really get a good look at her savior. What just happened felt like a scene from a James Bond movie. Now here she was, her forehead glistening with sweat, staring wide-eyed into the rugged, lined face of Dimitri Papandreou, one of the most notorious henchmen in the Greek cartel. She had only seen one photo of him and thought at the time that he was good-looking, but seeing him in person took her breath away.

"What the hell? You're Dimitri Papandreou. What are you *doing* here?"

"I've been assigned to protect you, Miss Boukamp. They want to take you out. Those two guys in the lobby? You're their number one threat. The cartel will protect Merkovitch at all costs and you must know they have jackals everywhere.

If you don't do what I tell you, they *will* kill you – today. Understand?" he said in his heavy Mediterranean accent. It was so heavy that she had to listen carefully to understand his words.

"Oh, I know they want me gone, but I didn't know they'd be here this soon. Where are you taking me?" None of this was making sense that Dimitri would be her rescuer. *Who put him up to it?*

"To a secure place here in the hotel. You'll be heavily guarded but you'll have to stay in the suite. All your needs will be taken care of until this is over. It's my assignment to make sure you stay healthy and alive. Don't worry. It's all been set up."

Again, she listened carefully to make sure she understood him. Watching her face as she listened to him, he had no idea she would be this captivating. Under different circumstances, he would have pushed his sturdy, six foot frame up against her, pinned her wrists over her head and locked his lips on hers. But his job, his only job right now, was to keep her alive and he had given his word that he would.

When the elevator doors opened, there were four heavily armed guards dressed in black, waiting to escort them to the electronically coded private elevator leading up to Dimitri's suite. Once there, two of them went ahead and performed a sweep of the two-bedroom luxury penthouse. The other two stayed behind and scanned the hallway.

As Alicia entered the living room, she drew a sharp breath in. It was furnished in sky blue and seafoam green with gold accents everywhere and a sweeping view of Tunic Bay. She had never seen such exquisite chandeliers, each with the same teardrop shaped crystals. She was sure her jaw dropped as

Dimitri ushered her into the living room. "What the hell! Is this for real?"

"Yes, Miss Boukamp, and you can relax. You're safe now. Take a look around. Your bedroom is on the far end to the right. I've had my assistant purchase some clothes for you. He tried to think of everything you might want or need."

Looking around, she had a sense of safety and appreciated what he had done, but what she really wanted was to finish the job on Merkovitch. Children were dying every day. The clock was ticking.

"I've taken the liberty of ordering dinner. We'll have a meal and discuss what's going to happen next, Miss Boukamp. If you'd like to freshen up, you'll find everything you need in your bathroom."

Holding out his hand, palm up, and glaring into her eyes, he said, "Please relinquish your weapon for the duration of your stay. You won't need it. Besides, if you were to pull it on me, you would not win."

She was still having a little trouble understanding him through his accent, but his message was clear, and not wanting a gun battle herself, she followed his instructions and relinquished her Glock as he led the way to the bathroom.

It was magnificent. White marble with gold fixtures, illuminating a translucent seafoam green oval wash basin. The clear glass shower was lined with pale green and gold marble tiles and gold shower heads. One upper and lower on one end and one upper on the other end. There was even a bidet next to the toilet. Her first thought was that the Greeks had nothing but money and power, as evidenced by this decadent suite.

When she returned to the living room, she told Dimitri she was going to take a quick shower before dinner. He agreed that might be a good idea to help her relax and showed her the towel warmer rack and how to switch it on. When he opened the narrow louvered door next to the shower, there was an assortment of white plush robes, three short and two long. "For your convenience," he said with a slight smile.

She showered and changed into a lavender sweater and jeans, shaking her head at how both fit perfectly. Whoever had done the clothes shopping seemed to know all about her physical form. That in itself was enough to unnerve any woman.

Their dinner was being delivered just as she returned to the living room. The presentation was divine. A starched white tablecloth trimmed with battenburg lace, two gold candlesticks, golden plate chargers and utensils, and a bouquet of six yellow roses in a cut crystal vase.

All of a sudden she felt grossly underdressed as Dimitri pulled out her chair to seat her. He had changed into a crisp, white linen shirt, sleeves rolled up to his elbows that highlighted his sun-kissed skin and deep brown eyes. As he leaned over the table to light the candles, she caught a whiff of his mellow fragrance.

"Dimitri, this is all very nice, but we need to talk about what's going on here. I want to know who assigned you to get me out of that mess downstairs."

"We will talk about all of that, Miss Boukamp, I assure you, but first red or white?" he asked, holding up a bottle of wine in each hand. She shook her head and rolled her eyes as she pointed to the bottle of red. As he poured, his eyes danced, his lips curling into a sly smile. "May I call you Alicia?"

"Oh, dammit Dimitri, I want to talk about Merkovitch right now and I really don't care what you call me. When this is all over, all I want is my sanity back."

He laughed out loud at her incredulous attitude. She was certainly scrappy. He knew, based on what he read in her dossier, that he was dealing with a determined woman. One that could be a loose cannon. He also knew that the human mind is the scariest place of all, but he had to get inside of hers if his rescue plan was going to work.

Not wanting to make him mad, Alicia casually asked when their meal was nearly over, if they could discuss the details that led to her rescue. Dimitri understood her curiosity and confirmed that he'd be willing to give her more information when they were finished eating. Now at least she felt like she was getting somewhere, just not as quickly as she wanted. Why, all of a sudden, was she getting the feeling that they were on some sort of bizarre date?

"Dimitri, I need to ask you a serious question. Is there a price on my head?" Dimitri looked up from his plate at her question and nodded in the affirmative. Then silence, which confirmed what she was thinking.

"Well? Are you going to tell me what it is or not?" He scooted his chair back from the table and crossed his arms across his broad chest, staring into her eyes. It was a grim look, revealing a hint of sadness. Dimitri was known as the "handler" in cases like this. Part of his job was to read people and he was good at it. Yet, in his 14 years of experience with the rescue team, he had never been exposed to someone like Alicia. Most of his rescues were greasy, sleazy men who didn't have a heart for saving anyone but themselves. It was different with her. What wasn't included in her dossier was the level of compassion for the children she was determined to free from bondage. Without it being spoken, they both knew that some of the children were also being sex-trafficked. That was the main reason Dimitri volunteered to take Alicia's rescue case.

"Yes, Alicia. There's a high price – $15,000,000 – which those two men in the lobby would undoubtedly split if they were to bring you in alive. But I'm not going to let them collect. Do you understand?"

Alicia's heart was pounding as the gravity of the situation sunk in. The price on her head was staggering, and she knew the men in the lobby would stop at nothing to get their hands on that fortune. However, the perseverance in her rescuer's voice gave her a glimmer of hope. She couldn't afford to let fear paralyze her now. It was time to fight back with everything she had, for the sake of the innocent children.

When Dimitri's phone rang, he excused himself to take the call, leaving Alicia to wonder what could be happening. When he returned several minutes later, his smile made her heart skip a beat. "It's done. Both assassins have been eliminated," he revealed, his expressive eyes sparkling with relief and pride.

Alicia couldn't help but feel overwhelmed with gratitude. "Dimitri, I don't know how you did it, but I want to thank you. You saved my life, and I'll be forever in your debt. But I have work to do. Can I go back home now?" she asked, her voice trembling with emotion.

"You can, if that's what you want. Or you could stay here, take a breather, and enjoy the luxuries this city has to offer.

Now that you're safe, perhaps you'd like to explore some of the sights with me? I've never been here before." Dimitri's heart raced as he made the offer, hoping Alicia would agree. He couldn't deny his growing admiration and wanted nothing more than to spend a little more time with her.

Blushing, she said, "Oh my! Mr. Papandreou, are you asking me out on a date?" Alicia teased, her eyes shining with delight.

"Just say yes, Ms. Boukamp. Just say yes," Dimitri replied, his heart swelling with anticipation.

Alicia rose from her seat, her eyes filled with excitement as she responded, "Yes, Dimitri, I'd like that. But there's just one thing I want in return – a conversation to find out what makes Dimitri Popandreou tick, because I have questions. Lots of them. Do we have a deal?"

There it was again. The incorrigible side of her he had been warned about. Dimitri couldn't help but feel a surge of warmth as he approached her, extending his hands. As their fingers touched, he winked and agreed, "Deal."

RED THUNDERBIRD

The day Erika turned 40 was also President's Day, so she threw a small party for a few of the people she worked with and a couple of her closest friends. The guys had a football game on TV, sitting around having a few beers, waiting for the food to be ready. The women were in the kitchen putting the finishing touches on an early dinner. Typical scenario.

Erika went into the living room to clean up some of the glasses, napkins, and paper plates when she saw a commercial for a local Ford dealership. It was advertising a President's Day blow-out sale on new Thunderbirds. The red one caught her eye immediately, stopping her dead in her tracks. As she moved closer to the TV to get a better look, one of the guys laughed and said, "Hey, Erika! We can't see through 'ya." His comment left her unfazed. She was mesmerized, picturing herself behind the wheel of the fire engine red beauty.

"That's it!" she shrieked. "I've never been able to buy a new car on my own, but I'm gonna buy that car *today*. Who wants to volunteer to drive me to the dealership?"

"Are you serious?" Fred asked.

"Yea, so serious that we need to eat and get down there. They're open till 8:00 and it's 3:30 now. I really want that car."

Fred quickly agreed to drive her, thinking that if she changed her mind and didn't buy the car for some reason, they could just come back to her place. No problem. He had a secret crush on her and wanted to play a part in her new adventure.

Erika had never had it easy, yet always worked hard to get ahead. She figured out that life was an obstacle course but never gave up. Many times, as she and her sister were growing up in a one parent household, her mother repeatedly preached that money didn't grow on trees.

One day, she decided it was time to break that poverty proclamation. Having an imagined conversation with her mother, she said, "Mom, how dare you make me afraid to live! That stops now!"

Fast forward to her 40th birthday. She had butterflies in her stomach as she and Fred approached the salesman at the dealership. But the butterflies turned to glee when she spotted *that* car on the showroom floor. Upon seeing his name tag, Erika, who was capable of being assertive when needed, confidently said, "Bill, I'd really like to take that red one for a test drive." As Bill assessed her, he wondered if she had the necessary credit rating to finance a vehicle like this. The final price tag for the car, including all costs, came to $24,380.

Trying to dissuade her, he replied, "I need to let you know that this particular Bird has a five-speed transmission with a turbocharger. That's a lot of power. Have you ever driven a stick shift?"

"Look, I understand you want to make sure I won't screw up the car and I can appreciate that. However, I learned to drive on a '34 Ford pickup when I was in high school. The engine was so souped up that when I let the clutch out too fast, the back wheels spun. Can we go on that test drive now?"

Bill grinned at her persistence and went off to get the keys and move the car off the showroom floor. While he was in the back office, she and Fred walked around the red beauty, opened the doors and sat inside. She noticed the sun roof, inhaled the smell of the mellow gray leather upholstery, and the dash that resembled an airplane cockpit. Wow!

With Bill in the passenger seat, Erika drove out of the lot, made the turn onto Hampshire Blvd., cruised along for a few blocks and then said, "I'd like to take it on the freeway. Are you OK with that?"

Bill had been watching the whole time and felt certain, by the way she shifted gears, that she knew how to drive. How she knew when to down-shift as they approached the stoplight, and when to shift out of first gear as she accelerated.

"Sure. Let's do it. Take a left at the next intersection. I know a shortcut." Once on the freeway, Erika punched it and that's when the turbo kicked in. Just the sound of it made her giddy. In her mind, this car was already hers. Which is exactly what happened when they finalized the paperwork. Bill had it washed and detailed while doing so, and then handed her the keys. Fred was impressed by the way she handled the whole transaction from start to finish. Just another reason, he thought, to admire this woman.

Not long after her purchase, her older sister, Debbie, came to town to check out her new wheels. She beamed with pride at what her kid sister had done. Erika told her to get in and they'd take it out in the country for a spin. "If you're nice, Deb, I'll even let you drive it," she smirked.

As she drove the two lane road, her sister, who shared her background, sat beside her, sharing her joy and understanding the significance of this moment. They both knew that this car represented more than just a material possession; it was a symbol of their resilience and determination to overcome their childhood poverty mindset.

But, as they rounded a sharp, hilly curve in the road, a car suddenly appeared in their lane, heading straight for them. Panic set in as Erika realized the unavoidable danger. She attempted to swerve, but the back end of her beloved Thunderbird hit the gravel on the shoulder, nearly sending them off the road into a hazardous drop.

Just as all hope seemed lost, an unseen force intervened, guiding the rear end of the car back onto the road, narrowly avoiding the oncoming vehicle. The sudden turn of events left Erika and Debbie speechless, but grateful for the mysterious force that saved their lives.

At the next pull-out, Erika stopped the car, looked over at Debbie, let out a deep sigh and said, "You know what, Sis? I think we just gave our guardian angels a reason to have a drinking problem." Laughing nervously, Deb replied, "I think you're right. Maybe I should drive us home so they can take a break."

KARMA KARNIVAL

A fateful trip to a traveling carnival in the year 1444 A.D. began Morgana's descent into the darkness. It was her 18th birthday when her family took her there for what they thought would be a day of celebration and merriment. But fate stepped in and she encountered the unscrupulous sorceress, Madame Zara.

Zara was a mysterious woman, rumored to possess knowledge of esoteric and supernatural attachments. Intrigued by her reputation, Morgana decided to have her fortune told. As Madame Zara peered into the crystal ball, she saw a darkness within Morgana's soul – a thirst for power and control that had yet to be awakened.

Recognizing the potential within the young girl, Madame Zara tantalized her, "I can show you how to live a life beyond your wildest dreams, my dear. All you have to do is perform the tasks that I'll teach you."

Morgana found what she said enticing and wanted to know more. That's when Zara began grooming Morgana in the ways of the ancient dark arts, revealing the secrets of manipulation and control. Under her nefarious guidance, Morgana honed her skills, quickly becoming proficient in the art of casting spells and conjuring curses, potions, and all kinds of black magic.

As Morgana's powers grew, so did her ambition. She soon became obsessed with the pursuit of more power, using her newfound abilities to manipulate those around her, including her unsuspecting family members. The innocence of her youth was now consumed by her lust for power, transforming her into the Wicked Witch Morgana, feared and reviled by all who knew her.

Driven by an insatiable greed, she relentlessly cast spells to manipulate the lives of others, twisting them to her malicious will and instigating chaos in their very existence. Yet, unbeknownst to her, the ancient law of karma had long presided over the land, guaranteeing that every action would ultimately reap its consequences.

The villagers lived in constant fear of Morgana, who now dwelled in a shadowy, secluded ancient castle, a short distance from the village at the top of Pegasus Peak. Her diabolical influence was felt throughout the village, as crops withered, livestock mysteriously disappeared, and strange illnesses plagued the townsfolk.

One day, a courageous young man named Henry, exasperated by the prolonged fear that had held the village hostage, decided that the time had come to put up resistance. Morgana had attempted more than once to capture Henry with her wicked spells, but her efforts failed, for his heart was pure and unyielding. Inspired by his strong will and undeniable spirit, the other villagers, who also had hearts of purity, came together in their determination to stand against the sinister force that plagued their once peaceful home.

"We are more powerful together and have no choice but to unite so as to end her reign of terror and destruction," he told them. They all agreed and armed themselves with pitchforks, torches, sticks, and whatever makeshift weapons they could find.

As twilight approached and the sun dipped below the horizon, Henry announced, "It's almost time. Let us each say a silent prayer of protection." All of the villagers bowed their heads and asked God to protect them, knowing that what they were facing was a demonic spirit.

They then gathered and marched towards Morgana's castle, torches blazing, their hearts filled with fear, but determined to take back the power of love that was theirs before the devil had taken over. They were met with fierce resistance, as the witch's dark magic conjured up all kinds of twisted creatures to protect her domain. However, the villagers fought with unwavering courage, their unity giving them strength and the power of the almighty that Morgana's minions couldn't overcome.

Ultimately, it was Henry who faced the evil witch herself as she stormed out of the castle, eyes as black as the night, her blood red lips hissing obscenities, "You stupid little peasants think you have power over me? Ha! Fools, all of you!"

But much to her surprise, four of the men came from behind, grabbing her arms and legs, taking her writhing body down to the ground. Now that she was subdued, Henry worked fast and managed to put her in a choke hold, plunging his knife blade into her neck, ending her reign of terror and freeing the village from her grip.

The villagers cheered as they watched her castle get struck by a huge rod of white light and crumble to the ground, her dark magic dissolving into clouds of black smoke. Karma had claimed her fortune and destiny. From that day forward, the village was free and prosperous, a testament to the universal law of whatever energy is given out will inevitably be returned.

THE CHERRY BOMB

From the time he was only four and drove his rickety pedal car three miles on the streets of town to the standpipe on the hill, Richie was a curious little fella. When his Mama found out what he did, she chastised him, hoping it would deter him from a repeat performance.

If you're thinking it worked, it didn't. Richie was the most curious boy in town and Mama knew she had her hands full. He wasn't the kind of kid that liked to stay in the house and do puzzles, read, play his harmonica, or build structures with his erector set. All of the things he used to do had been swept away by his insatiable curiosity for what might be 'out there.'

As Richie grew up, he did things like timing how long it took for an ice cream cone to melt and drip down to his elbow. And then there was the day he took his birthday present, an archery set, out in the front yard. But, instead of shooting arrows at the target, he laid down on the grass and shot them straight up into the sky, just because he wanted to see where they'd land when they came down. Mama wasn't thrilled when his uncle gave him that gift and really freaked out when a neighbor tattled on what he was doing with it. She took the archery set away and grounded him for a week.

"Richie, you know I have to go to work, so I *really* need you to mind me when I ask you to watch your sister until I get home. Do you understand?"

"Sure, Mom. I'll take her with me next time."

"What? Oh, no you won't, young man! Monica's only 9 and you're only 13. You may think you're hot stuff, but neither of you are old enough to be wandering around town on your own or shooting arrows into the sky."

Monica listened intently to the conversation, feeling a strong urge to share some information about Richie that her mother was unaware of. However, she decided to keep quiet, knowing that he would, most likely, retaliate against her later. Despite her young age, Monica was wise enough to recognize that Richie often managed to weasel out of consequences for his actions.

The Fourth of July was approaching and Mama was worried that Richie would take his lawn-mowing money and spend it all on fireworks, so she warned him about it.

"Richie, I don't mind if want you to spend some of your money on fireworks this year, but please don't go overboard, OK? And no bottle rockets or cherry bombs."

"Mom, me and Jerry know how to use fireworks, so don't worry. We'll be careful. Besides, Uncle Larry already said we could do them at his place."

Uncle Larry was the same person who gave Richie the bow and arrows, and was a bit of a daredevil himself, so that didn't make Mama feel much better. He, his wife, and two boys owned a quarter horse ranch on the outskirts of town. There were no close neighbors, so Larry felt like the fireworks wouldn't pose any danger.

BETWEEN YESTERDAY AND TOMORROW

The Fourth of July came, so Mama, Monica, Richie, and Jerry went to the ranch for the festivities. Aunt Kathy made her special red, white, and blue ribbon cake, adorned with coconut flakes, fresh blueberries, and strawberries. Uncle Larry had three full racks of ribs already cooking on the grill when they arrived. The horses were all secure in the barn.

Everyone had a grand time. The fireworks were safely deployed with supervision. Around the picnic table, there were smiles and laughter, which were followed by the singing of the National Anthem, the family's annual tribute to liberty. After it was all cleaned up, Mama, Monica, and the boys said their thanks and goodbyes and headed home.

The next morning as Mama was going out the door to work, she thanked Richie for behaving himself with the fireworks. Curious, she asked, "Did you use them all?"

"I think so, Mom. I'll check my backpack and if there's any left, I'll get rid of them." What she didn't know was that he had secretly saved a cherry bomb.

Monica saw it when she put a baggie of leftover ribs in his backpack before they left the ranch, but was afraid to say anything. So after Mama left for work, she asked Richie what he was going to do with it. With his usual grin, he said, "You'll find out."

He waited until Grandpa came to pick up Monica for her dentist appointment, grabbed his backpack from the closet, and pulled out the cherry bomb. With the devil on one shoulder and an angel on the other, he thought, "Should I do it?" A case of nerves was setting in, which made him have to go to the bathroom. He put the seat up and started his stream, his curiosity asking what would happen if he lit the cherry bomb and flushed it down the toilet. The little dancing demon on his left shoulder was laughing with glee, while the angel on his right cried out in pain.

"Please, please, Richie. Don't do it! Your Mama will have to pay for the damage. Don't forget the sacrifices she's made for you. Is this how you want to repay her?"

The dancing devil went silent. The angel won. And so did Richie. Picturing his Mama's loving face, with a tear trickling down his cheek, he tossed the cherry bomb into the trash and then flushed the toilet.

SOMEDAY SEDONA

I saw you only once,
    Yet, in my soul, I've known you before,
    There you drift, keeping watch,
    Beckoning me to your door.
    Many souls have walked your streets,
    Climbed your jagged banks,
    Knowing the awe of your seduction,
    And feeling the peace of thanks.
    In dreams I walk your ancient paths,
    And know the weight of time.
    Your secrets whispered through the years,
    Draw me closer to the climb.
    The day will dawn when we unite,
    My spirit and your glow.
    I'll stand where many have before,
    And let your essence flow.
    For in your depths my soul shall see,
    The substance it's been searching for.
    Embrace me, my Sedona,
    In waves of love and more.
    My time will come for you to
    Share with me your bliss.
    I hear your whispers,

Know the breath of your kiss.
Someday Sedona, I'll come to you.

SERAPHINA

Bridget had just turned 16 and loved to take the shortcut by the river as she walked home after school. The autumn afternoon light made the river look like sparkling sapphires. One day, stopping to look at it, she noticed a bright, golden glow coming from behind her. As she looked to see what it was, her eyes widened with fear.

But before she could turn and run, she heard a soft, soothing voice, "Don't be afraid, dear one. I would never hurt you. I'm Seraphina, your guardian angel. Are you ready to hear the advice I have for you?" Bridget immediately noticed that Seraphina didn't ask if she *wanted* to hear it; she asked if she was ready.

Confused but curious, Bridget asked, "Why are you asking me this?"

She peered into Bridget's eyes without blinking and said, "Because what you're ready to hear is that you have a special purpose, and what I'm about to say will help you for the rest of your life. My advice for you, beautiful soul, is to learn certain things if you want to fulfill your dharma and be happy:"

"Dharma? What the heck is *that?*" Bridget asked, still a bit nervous that she might be dreaming.

Seraphina, in a reassuring voice, explained that the word dharma comes from Sanskrit, the ancient language of India.

"Dharma is part of the cosmic order of things, the rightful duty of every human being living on earth to live their purpose. Now, if you're ready, I'll share what you need to know. Let's begin with a bit of advice about other people, OK?" Awestruck, all Bridget could do was nod in agreement.

"The first thing you must know is that you can't make real friends with false people. They rely on their ego more than their intuition. Real friends, however, are authentic, trustworthy, and sincere. Real friends are the ones who accept and appreciate you for who you are, without judgment or pretense. Genuine friendships are built on trust, support, and understanding, which allows you to grow and learn from one another. On the other hand, false people are usually inconsistent in their behaviors and actions, making it difficult to form a genuine bond between you and them. Their relationships tend to be superficial, based on appearances and social status rather than mutual understanding and shared experiences."

It was a lot to take in, but Bridget paid close attention and began to see that there were people in her life who were not trustworthy and told her only what they thought she wanted to hear.

"But how will I know who's who?" Bridget asked. The angel smiled tenderly and gave her this advice: "Sit back and observe, dear girl. They will show you by their actions, not necessarily their words. And remember, not everything needs your immediate reaction."

Looking back on a recent experience, Bridget nodded her head, recalling a secret she had shared with a friend about a boy she had a crush on. The next day her friend had posted about it on social media. Bridget felt betrayed.

Seraphina continued with, "Always trust your inner voice. If something doesn't feel right about a person or situation, don't waste your precious energy trying to deny it. Your intuition will never lie to you. Build self-awareness by understanding that your relationship with yourself is the most important one you'll ever have, second only to the one you have with your Creator."

Bridget asked, "What happens if I find out that I can't trust someone and don't want to be friends with them anymore?"

"My dear sweet soul, the older you get, the less you'll feel the need to be in relationships where someone doesn't value your worth, understand, or accept you. I see your heart and want you to know that you're doing enough even if it doesn't feel like it, so please don't lower your standards."

Bridget was antsy, recalling a situation with a friend that made her feel afraid, but she never let anyone know what happened. Based on what Seraphina had already told her, she felt safe enough to ask about it.

"I have to ask you a question. A couple of weeks ago, one of my closest friends told me that if I'd write some nasty words on a piece of paper and slip it into someone's backpack, she'd give me five dollars. She wanted me to write things like slut, whore, and a word I don't even want to say out loud. I told her no, and she said she'd never talk to me again. What should I do?" Seraphina saw the tears welling up in Bridget's eyes.

With a deep sigh, Seraphina replied, "You did the right thing by saying no to that girl. When someone tells you to do something that you know is wrong or will hurt another, you must ask yourself if it's something you want done to you. Furthermore, if people want to put you into that kind of situation, realize that they are *not* your people. They're coming from an unhealed place. Energy vampires are everywhere, so you must learn to set firm boundaries."

Before Seraphina continued with her advice, she beamed pure, unconditional love directly into Bridget's heart. The smile and look of peace on Bridget's face was unmistakable. It had reached her.

Seraphina continued in a soft, loving voice, "A few words of advice now about being in love, young one. It will happen for you, and when it does, please remember this: if someone loves you the way they claim, their actions will show it. Their actions will consistently demonstrate it. They will prioritize your happiness, respect your boundaries, and support your growth. Love is not merely an emotion, but an active choice to care for and invest time and energy into another person. You'll see it by tangible actions. Just know that you'll have wins and losses in relationships of all kinds. It's part of the human experience. But always remember that a healthy relationship is one in which both people support each other's personal growth."

Seraphina could tell by the way Bridget was looking at her that she was taking it all in, word for word.

"My final piece of advice is to live for the moments you can't put into words. You may not know what that means right now, but someday you will. If you want to feel rich, count all the things in your life that money can't buy. Like when you see the azure blue of that river, a high drama sunset that takes your breath away, or how your newborn baby looks into your eyes for the first time. And lastly, my dear Bridget, hold onto your childlike faith. Forgive everyone who hurts you. Forgiveness isn't for them. It's for you and it will set you free. I have to go now, but I'm always with you. Remember, love transcends physical boundaries, so even when I'm not there with you physically like you see me now, I am always with you in spirit. Whenever you need guidance or comfort, take a moment to quiet your mind, call out to me and ask for answers. The answers may come in various forms – a sudden realization or a meaningful encounter. Trust that these signs are my way of communicating with you, and be patient for their arrival. Rest assured, my love for you is eternal, dear Bridget. I will stand by your side until the end of time. Oh, and one last thing ... when you see a white feather, it's me."

FAMILY SECRETS

Shannon had built a life full of love and memories, surrounded by her family and friends. She was the youngest of two siblings, with her brother, David, three years her senior. They hadn't always been close growing up, but still shared a bond that only siblings would understand.

David, from the time he was a teenager, was always hustling to get ahead. Their mother, Cecilia, idolized him. In her eyes, he was a shining star and could do no wrong. Shannon felt slighted when Cecilia boasted about David, so she tried hard to be a loving, caring daughter in hopes that Cecilia would recognize her efforts.

Cecilia and their father, Wayne, were divorced when Shannon was six, so she only had little glimpses of what life was like as a family. There were pictures, though, one of which was her favorite. She was wearing a yellow organza dress, sitting on a pony with Wayne's arm around her, smiling.

When Shannon was 10, she began asking her mother questions about Wayne. Cecilia brushed it off, saying that he was lazy and didn't want to provide for them, so it was better that they went their separate ways. Shannon longed to find out more, so she brought it up with her grandmother and got the same answer. The abandonment in Shannon's heart became a stumbling block. But with David being older, she thought he might remember something that could provide her with answers, so she asked him what he remembered about their dad. He told her of the incident when Wayne arrived at their house one weekend to pick them up. However, he completely ignored David, who eagerly approached him with open arms. Instead, Wayne focused solely on Shannon, as if David was invisible. David, hurt by the snub, quietly walked away.

As they became adults and had families of their own, Shannon often wondered if Cecilia was hiding something. But caught up in a busy life with her husband and children, she never pursued it further.

Wayne remarried and had three more children. His new life no longer included her and David at all. No one in the family ever mentioned him again. As the years passed, Shannon and David both moved to different parts of the country, pursuing careers, raising children, and living normal lives. But Cecilia continued to comment on how well David was doing and how much money he was making. Shannon could never recall a time when her mom said that about her, even though she had a thriving career as V.P. for a large tech firm in Salt Lake City. She never called her mother out for it, but it seeped into her soul.

With the kids grown and off on their own, Shannon and her husband relocated to the Southwest and had just moved into a seven acre property. David was living in the same area so it made sense to live close to their mom, who was getting up in years.

One day, while sitting around their mom's patio table talking, Shannon looked at David and honed in on the cleft in his chin. It had always been there but suddenly a light bulb went off. No one in their family, including their uncles and grandpa, had a cleft. She brought it up to her husband later that evening. "Honey, maybe I'm crazy but I was looking at David this afternoon and the cleft in his chin really stood out to me. And he doesn't look like anyone in the family. He has green eyes and no one else does." Hubby agreed that it was odd, too, but nothing else was said about it. However, the thought kept nagging her.

One day when she was cleaning out a file cabinet, she noticed the folder with Wayne's Navy discharge papers and a letter his second wife, LaVerne, had written after he passed away at age 66. LaVerne wanted Shannon to have them, but when she received them, she filed them away with barely a glance. Now, she decided to really read the letter. It was full of remorse that Wayne had over the years that he didn't stay in touch with her and David.

Shannon's life was about to take an unexpected twist as she delved into the mysterious depths of her family's past. Upon reading her father's discharge papers, she discovered a startling revelation. Her dad had been deployed in Guam when her mother conceived David. The timeline matched, leaving her in a state of shocked silence. Her mind raced with unanswered questions, the most pressing of which was *who was David's biological father?*

Overwhelmed with the need for answers, Shannon initially intended to confront her mother right away. However, her husband advised her to seek confirmation from her uncle William first, hoping he could provide some clarity. During a tense lunch meeting, Shannon looked directly into William's eyes and posed the question, "Is my father David's father?"

William's emotional reaction, as he choked up and cried, confirmed the devastating truth. He explained that Shannon's father had agreed to keep her mother's secret because he loved her. Together, they decided to have another child. Apparently Cecilia and Wayne wanted to have a child together, thinking it would keep them together. It didn't. Right then Shannon realized why her mother treated her as second best. She was the sacrificial lamb.

Shannon decided to confront her mother about what she had learned. To her surprise, Cecilia admitted everything. David's real father had been her lover while Wayne was overseas. When she became pregnant, she confessed everything to Wayne in a letter before he got home from Guam. They agreed to keep the secret, as did the entire family, to protect David and Shannon. Cecilia never told the other man that he had a son.

Shannon was furious that the whole family knew – everyone but her and David. "Mom, how could you do this to David and me? I can't believe that I'm just now finding this out. How dare you keep him away from his real father! Why didn't you tell him when he became an adult? He could have accepted it."

In tears now, Cecilia answered, "I was afraid he wouldn't love me if he found out what I did."

"Really, Mother? You're making this all about you when your own son doesn't know who his biological father is? You are so damn selfish! I want you to tell me … who is it?" What's his name and where can I find him?"

Cecilia got up and stood nose to nose with Shannon, "No, not after all this time. It would hurt him deeply. I've carried the guilt with me all these years and I'll have to take it to my grave. And if you tell him, I'll never speak to you again." Shannon was enraged and stormed out of the house, slamming the door behind her.

Anger, betrayal, and confusion consumed her. She cried all the way back to her house, asking God why she had to be the one who found out this secret. And why now? What was she supposed to do with this? She struggled to come to terms with the fact that she and David's entire lives had been built on a lie.

Deep down she knew it would only hurt David to know the truth. So after searching her soul, the answer came. She wouldn't tell him. But knowing the truth, she finally realized why he had always sought validation from outside of himself. At the soul level, he must have known.

David developed cancer and passed away when he was 66, but for the previous eight months, he and Shannon got to experience a connection like they never had before. She learned that the bonds of family were not defined by blood, but by the love, trust, and acceptance they shared with each other.

David passed, never knowing the truth. Later, his wife told Shannon of a comment David made a couple of years before, "My dad died at 66 and I probably will, too." Shannon sobbed and let out a slow, deep breath, saying a silent prayer that David's real father had been there to greet him when he transitioned to the other side.

THE MONKFISH CAFE

Franklin Bay, renowned for its dramatic cliffs, pristine beaches, and scenic hiking trails, attracted nature enthusiasts and photographers alike from all over the west coast.

Brendon was a photographer for a local travel magazine, who never got tired of photographing the harbor seals, sea lions, and various birds, including an occasional blue heron. One of the harbor seals always made him laugh because when she saw him point the camera, she would tilt her head and strike a pose. He decided to give her a nickname – Posing Polly.

Ready for a lunch break after shooting 68 images, he arrived at the bustling Monkfish Cafe. It was pretty crowded with people waiting for a table, but he noticed an empty seat at the bar. He sat down next to a peculiar-looking man, seemingly lost in thought. Intrigued by the man's puzzling demeanor, he decided to strike up a conversation. The man, who introduced himself as Thomas, was a retired sea captain with a wealth of stories about his adventures and the rich history of Point Mariner. While chatting over lunch, Thomas revealed a long-held secret about a hidden treasure buried somewhere near the lighthouse, dating back to the 1800's.

"Wow, Thomas! Do you think that's really true or is it just an urban legend that's been embellished over the years?"

Thomas chuckled and replied, "You're not the first person to question it. But, yes I do believe it. I was shown an old letter and captain's log from the Mystic Mirage, one of the ships that sailed these waters around 1855 before heavy squalls took her under. There was no map, but the coordinates were there. Barely readable."

Brendon, enthralled by the prospect of uncovering the hidden treasure and photographing everything about it, asked if he could join forces with Thomas to uncover the truth behind the legend. Thomas hesitated but had taken a liking to Brendon's inquisitive nature, so he finally agreed. Little did they know their quest would lead them to uncover not only the lost treasure, but also the dark secrets lurking beneath the picturesque depths of Point Mariner.

As Brendon and Thomas investigated deeper into the mystery, they discovered that the legend of the lost treasure was intertwined with a sinister plot. They unearthed old parchment documents and maps that pointed to a hidden network of underground tunnels directly beneath the Point, which had been used for smuggling during the Prohibition Era. Intrigued by their findings, they decided to explore the tunnels themselves.

Brendon was concerned and asked, "What do you think we'll find in there? I'm a little nervous about this, aren't you?"

Thomas, with a slight groan, admitted, "Yep, but we've come this far and can't turn back now. If we do, we'll always wonder."

They met the next morning at the cafe, with all the gear they would need for their exploration. As they ventured into the darkness, going deeper into the tunnels, they stumbled upon a series of cob-webbed chambers filled with long-forgotten relics and artifacts. Among them was a dusty, ancient book containing cryptic writings and illustrations that hinted at the treasure's location. With renewed determination, they pressed on, deciphering the clues as they went, leading them deeper into the caverns.

Their journey eventually led them to a hidden chamber adorned with ornate carvings and a massive iron door. They were shocked that the door was so easy to open. And even more shocked when they discovered the lost treasure. A trove of gold, jewels, and priceless Asian artifacts from a bygone era.

However, their joy was short-lived as they soon found themselves confronted by the cave people, descendants of the original treasure hunters, who had been guarding the secret for generations. Brendon and Thomas were more than a little frightened. But the cave people were not aggressive and ultimately admitted that it was time to give up hoarding the treasure. They were tired of living underground and for what? To guard something that was doing them no good?

As they emerged from the tunnels, they found themselves in a world forever changed by their discovery. The secrets they had uncovered would have to be exposed, and would shake the foundations of Point Mariner. Their lives and the lives of the cave people would never be the same.

But the primary thing Brendon and Thomas learned that day is that perseverance is the undeniable spirit that drives all people to overcome obstacles and achieve their goals, no matter what challenges they may face in uncovering the truth.

COLD NOSES

Dogs, with love pure unbending,
   In their eyes, human hearts they're tending.
   Our four-legged friends, faithful and true,
   Their love for us, each day renews.
   With wagging tails and joyous leaps,
   They greet us, no sorrows they keep.
   Their loyalty, a bond so strong,
   A love as vast as life's own song.
   With cold noses, a gentle touch,
   A sign of their affection, a little nudge.
   In every glance, their love they show,
   A connection that only we and they know.
   Through trials and tribulations,
   Their love remains, no hesitation.
   In moments both light and dark,
   Our furry friends, a gentle spark.
   And when we're lost in sorrow's trap,
   They lend an ear, snuggle on our lap.
   Their love, a beacon in the night,
   A comforting presence, a guiding light.
   So here's to the dogs, our loyal mates,
   Whose love transcends all bounds and gates.
   With cold noses and hearts so warm,

BETWEEN YESTERDAY AND TOMORROW

Their love, a treasure, forever adored.

THE SLEEPING BEAST

Allison sat at the edge of the cliff, her feet dangling over the abyss, the wind howling around her. The sun was just beginning to set, casting shadows on the jagged rocks below. She watched the shadows grow longer, the world slowly sinking into twilight. It was a magical sight, but it did little to ease the turmoil in her heart. She prayed, "God, show me what you want me to do."

Everyone knew her as the kindest, most loving person around. She volunteered at the local soup kitchen, read books to the elderly in Shady Oaks Senior Center, and even helped her neighbors with their yard work. Her bright smile and warm hugs were a beacon of hope in a world that often seemed cold and indifferent.

But there was another side to Allison, a side that few had ever seen. A side that was born from the darkness she had endured in her past. A side that was fierce, unyielding, and as dangerous as the jagged rocks far below.

Allison's journey to this cliff began when she was just a child. Her father and stepmother were alcoholics, and their home was a constant battlefield of violence and neglect. She learned to be self-sufficient at a young age, scavenging for food and clothing, and avoiding the brutal fights that erupted between her parents. Inside, she she was always in fight or flight mode.

It was during one of these times that her stepmother, in a drunken stupor, accidentally set fire to their home, the flames quickly engulfing the tiny clapboard house. Allison found herself trapped, the heat and smoke suffocating her little body. She had never felt so helpless, so alone. But just as she was about to give up, a firefighter burst through the flames and scooped her up to safety.

That firefighter, a man named Jack, became Allison's guardian angel. Child Services removed her from her parents, so Jack and his wife volunteered to take care of her. They welcomed her into their home, and for the first time in her life, she experienced the warmth and safety of a loving family. Jack's kindness and strength inspired her, and she vowed to one day become just like him.

As she grew up, it became apparent that her life before with her parents was dismal and that's where her darkness came from. It was inside her, a beast that had been born from the traumas of her past. It was a side of her that she struggled to control, a side that threatened to consume the goodness.

One day, while serving meals at the soup kitchen, Allison encountered a man who reminded her of her father. He was drunk and aggressive, and began to harass an older man, a disabled veteran, calling him nasty names. Allison's blood boiled, and the beast within her stirred. She felt a primal rage building inside her, a desire to protect the vulnerable and punish the wicked.

Without thinking, she screamed profanities and lunged at the man, her fists flying. She unleashed a torrent of fury upon him, her strength fueled by years of pain and anger. The man was no match for her, and he soon crumbled to the ground, defeated.

As Allison stood over him, her chest heaving with rage, she heard Jack's voice in her head saying, "Allison, stop! This is NOT who you are." That's when she realized she had become the very thing she despised. She had allowed the darkness within her to take control, and in doing so, had become an angry monster.

From that day forward, Allison vowed to never let the beast within her take control again. She would channel her strength and resilience into acts of kindness and love, using her pain as a catalyst for good. She would become the embodiment of the light that had saved her from the darkness, a beacon of hope for those who had lost their way.

And so, Allison found herself sitting on the edge of the cliff, the wind howling around her. She stared into the abyss, contemplating the depths of her soul. She admitted that the beast within her was still there, sleeping beneath the surface, waiting for the right moment to awaken. But she wasn't afraid. She knew that her kindness was not a sign of weakness, but rather a testament to her strength. She had faced the darkness and survived, and would continue to do so with God's help, one act of love at a time.

Allison stood up and turned her back on the abyss. She knew that her journey was far from over, but she also knew that she wasn't alone. She had the love and support of her rescuer, Jack and his family, her friends, and the strength of her own indomitable spirit.

Allison walked away from the cliff, her heart filled with hope and determination. The beast within her may have been sleeping, yet she knew it wasn't dead. But, she was sure that, as long as she continued to choose kindness and love, it would have no voice and never reawaken again.

REDEMPTION

After graduating from college in California, Ethan moved to New York in his early twenties to take a new job as a software engineer at a well-known high tech firm. He was known for his hard work, dedication, and ambition, but there was a dark secret that haunted him. Ethan had shunned his mother, Olivia, when he was just twelve years old, after his father had filled his head with lies about her.

Ethan's father, a manipulative and cunning man, had painted Olivia as a heartless and selfish woman who had abandoned him, shaming her constantly by the untrue stories he told. In fact, that's how he won legal custody of his son. Ethan, being young and vulnerable, had believed every word his father said. He cut off all contact with his mother and refused to even acknowledge her existence. But from somewhere deep inside he had a knowing that his mother always loved him. It's just that she had made some poor choices and his father had taken advantage of that to make her look like a monster.

Years went by, and Ethan's life seemed to be going well. He had a stable job, a loving girlfriend, and a promising future. However, the guilt he felt for disowning his mother was always in the back of his mind, gnawing at him like a cancer. His girlfriend, Beth, had on many occasions pleaded with him to reach out to Olivia and start a conversation, but he refused. He was afraid too much time had gone by and worried about the backlash he would experience if his father found out.

After a stressful day at work, putting out one fire after another, Ethan was tired and thought he'd stop off for a beer before going home. He called Beth. "Hey, honey, I'm gonna grab a beer with a couple of the guys. It's been a rough day." She replied, "Fine, but don't be too late, OK?" He and his buddies had a good time, cracking jokes and laughing about the crazy day.

When he was only a few blocks from the apartment, a drunk driver ran the red light at the intersection and slammed into Ethan's BMW, crushing him inside the car. As he lay dying in the wreckage, he suddenly found himself transported to a strange, ethereal place. It was here that he experienced a life review, where he was forced to relive all the major events of his life, but from the perspective of the people he had relationships with. As Ethan was shown the pain and suffering he had caused his mother, he felt a deep sense of remorse and sorrow. He saw how his mother had tried desperately to reconnect with him, only to be stonewalled as he met her with coldness and rejection. He felt the anguish she went through as she watched her son slip away from her, all because of the lies he believed about her.

Ethan's life review also showed him the truth about his father. How he had manipulated and controlled him for his own selfish reasons. The lies his father had told him, filled with bitterness, were nothing more than a means to keep Ethan under his control, and to keep Olivia from having any influence in his life.

As Ethan's life review came to an end, he found himself back in the wreckage of the car. Miraculously, he had survived the accident, and was given a second chance at life. With his newfound knowledge and understanding, Ethan vowed to make amends for the pain he had caused his mother.

It took almost a year for him to recover from his injuries, and while doing so, he had a lot of time for introspection. Once he was feeling better, he enlisted the help of a private investigator. The P.I. tracked his mother down and Ethan reached out to her. Shocked and somewhat hesitant, she agreed to meet with him.

As they sat across from each other in a small coffee shop, Ethan poured out his heart, confessing his guilt and asking for her forgiveness. His mother, though cautious at first, eventually embraced him and forgave him for the years of pain and suffering he had caused her. She asked for his forgiveness, too, and with tears in their eyes, they both admitted that they had never stopped loving each other, even from a distance. Neither of them focused on the part Ethan's father had played in everything. Their healing had begun.

When he told her about the night he had the accident, she broke down sobbing, and after regaining her composure, told him what had happened to her that night – her whole body had begun shaking uncontrollably without any warning. It was at the same time the car crashed into Ethan.

Ethan's life changed dramatically after that day. He severed all ties with his father, knowing he had to eliminate the toxicity and yet forgive him. He began working on rebuilding the relationship with his mother. He came to understand the importance of family, love, and forgiveness, and vowed never to let lies and manipulation control his life again.

In time, Ethan and his mother grew closer, their bond becoming stronger than ever. Their lives took a new direction, filled with hope, love, and redemption. The lies that had once controlled Ethan were finally over, and he was free to live a life based on truth, honesty, and earnest caring.

Olivia had always yearned for a vacation in Hawaii, yet the steep cost was never in her budget. Two weeks before Mother's Day, a package arrived unexpectedly from Ethan. Inside, she discovered two first-class tickets to Maui and a note that read: "Aloha, Mom! Pack your bags. We have some lost time to make up for. With lots of love, Ethan."

PENDULUM SWINGS BOTH WAYS

The real estate market was booming in Dallas, so Mark was enjoying a prosperous year as a broker for a large, well known firm when he met his match. She was young, energetic, and wanted to make it to the top of her game. Her goal was to be the number one agent in the company.

Gwen was highly skilled at obtaining listings, sometimes to the detriment of the sellers, promising a quick sale which she didn't always accomplish. Mark counseled her on many occasions, warning that she was taking the wrong approach. He told her that he would always have her back, but only if she was honest with all parties involved in the transactions.

However, despite Mark's repeated warnings, Gwen's ambitions continued to drive her actions, leading her down a treacherous path. She began to forge documents, manipulate property values, and even engage in insider trading to secure lucrative deals. As her success skyrocketed, people started to question how she made it so quickly. Whispers of corruption began to circulate around Dallas and within the industry.

Mark, torn between loyalty to his protégé and his own moral compass, found himself at a crossroads. He knew that if he exposed Gwen's illicit activities, it could bring down the entire firm and ruin countless careers, including his own.

However, if he chose to remain silent, he would be complicit in her actions, find himself in legal proceedings, and the integrity of the real estate industry would continue to crumble.

Unfortunately, Gwen's activities only grew more nefarious. She began to bribe city officials and forge zoning permits, all in the name of securing the most sought-after properties for her clients. Mark, unable to bear the weight of his conscience any longer, and the evidence he had uncovered, finally decided to blow the whistle on her corrupt practices.

The fallout was catastrophic. The firm was implicated in the scandal, and countless careers were left in ruins. However, amidst the chaos, a glimmer of hope emerged. Mark's brave decision to expose corruption in the real estate field sparked a much-needed conversation about the importance of integrity and transparency in the industry.

Ultimately, the journey of Mark and Gwen served as a cautionary tale about the dangers of ambition and the importance of staying true to one's moral compass, even when the path forward seems uncertain. Gwen learned the hard way that, in business and in life, the pendulum always swings both ways.

ADSUM, I AM HERE

In the heart of ancient Rome, during the reign of Emperor Nero, young soldiers were tasked with guarding the city's walls. Each day, as the sun rose, they would take their positions and prepare for the roll call. The commanding officers, known as Legati, were responsible for overseeing military campaigns, leading troops into battle, and ensuring the smooth operation of the entire Roman military.

As Legati officers slowly rode their magnificent white horses, inspecting the line of soldiers, each warrior would call out proudly "Adsum!" meaning I am present, which signaled to Legati that they were ready to serve. Committed to their sentry duty, they never wavered.

But one day, with the morning temperature unusually hot, one of the officers noticed that a soldier didn't respond when called on. He shouted, "Soldier!" The young man still didn't respond and looked like he was going to faint. The officer dismounted and came closer. That's when the soldier moaned, collapsed, and keeled over.

The officer, a seasoned veteran named Gaius, removed the soldier's helmet, recognized that it was Marcus, the only nephew of Emperor Nero, and knew that time was of the essence. He made the decision to prioritize Marcus's life over protocol. He instructed his men to stay at their post while he took Marcus to the nearest medical facility, where they could provide the necessary care to save Nero's nephew.

The journey was perilous, with the heat of the day only intensifying as Gaius drove the chariot, and Marcus's condition continuing to deteriorate. When they finally arrived at the medical outpost, Gaius's heart raced with fear and uncertainty. Would they be too late?

The medical staff immediately went to work, administering fluids and cooling Marcus's body to bring down his fever. Gaius paced anxiously outside the treatment room, waiting for any news of his condition. Hours passed, and finally, a healer emerged with a weary but hopeful expression. "Your soldier is stable now," the healer informed Gaius, "but he will need considerable time to recover. It was a close call, however, we managed to bring his body temperature down and rehydrate him. He will be weak for some time, but he should make a full recovery."

Relief washed over Gaius, but he knew that the ordeal was far from over. He would have to face Nero and explain the situation, potentially risking his own career in the process. But as he looked at the unconscious Marcus, he knew that he had made the right decision – a life had been saved, and that was worth any consequence that might come his way.

In the days that followed, Gaius stood by Marcus's side as he slowly regained his strength. One morning as he entered the room, Marcus, in a barely audible whisper, said, one word, "Adsum." Gaius squeezed his hand, letting Marcus know he had been heard.

When the time came to face Nero, Gaius did so with a clear conscience, knowing that he had acted with integrity and honor. And in the end, Nero, moved by the depth of Gaius's loyalty and courage, chose to give him a promotion, recognizing that the preservation of life was more important than any military protocols.

Together, Gaius and Marcus emerged from the ordeal with a newfound bond, forged from adversity and the unwavering commitment to doing what was right, no matter the cost. And so, the legacy of "Adsum" lived on, a testament to the power of human compassion and the enduring spirit of Rome.

BETWEEN YESTERDAY AND TOMORROW

FROM HAREM TO PRISON

Leo lived in southern Nevada for most of his adult life. At 63, he was a rather charming, handsome guy, six feet, two inches tall, steel blue eyes, with sandy blond hair, slightly gray at the temples. Women's hearts fluttered everywhere he went. However, he had a wife, Lisa, who was the woman of his dreams. Or so he thought.

One day, Leo decided to spice up his life by engaging in a torrid affair with the next-door neighbor, the sultry 42 year-old Sophia. He thought he was being extremely careful, but fate had other plans.

As luck would have it, on an otherwise ordinary day, Lisa decided to surprise Leo by picking up some Chinese takeout and coming home early from work. She walked into their apartment and was greeted by the sight of her husband and Sophia tangled in each other's arms, their clothes scattered on the floor.

Lisa's eyes almost bulged out of her head in disbelief, and before Leo could come up with an excuse, she unleashed a torrent of obscenities that would make a sailor blush. As her adrenaline escalated, she then proceeded to throw everything in sight at the pair, including a large, heavy pewter vase that knocked Leo unconscious.

BETWEEN YESTERDAY AND TOMORROW

When he woke up, he was in the hospital with a bandage around his head and Lisa glaring at him from the corner of the room. He tried to apologize, but she was having none of it. He could see the look of determination on her face as she told him, "Our marriage is over and I'm moving out."

Dejected, Leo returned home to find that Lisa had taken everything, leaving behind only a note that read, "I hope your little escapade was worth it."

In the end, Leo learned the hard way that sometimes trying to have your cake and eat it, too, can lead to a whole lot of trouble, and a rather painful bump on the head. From that day on, he made a vow to himself that he would never cheat on anyone ever again, and he kept that promise - for at least a whole week.

As the news of Leo's misadventures spread through town, he became somewhat of a local legend. Men would often stop him in the streets and ask for his autograph, as if he was a famous athlete or movie star.

Heartbroken, Lisa subsequently learned that he had been cheating on her with multiple women, even swindling a couple of them out of a good sum of money. That discovery only compounded the betrayal and rejection she felt the day she discovered him in their apartment with Sophia.

In the process of filling out the divorce paperwork, Lisa was advised by her attorney to block her soon to be ex-husband everywhere, including his phone number, email, and social media accounts. Leo got the picture and began checking his snail mail every day, secretly hoping for some correspondence from Lisa, but instead there was a mysterious letter in the mailbox. It was an invitation to join an exclusive organization

– The Cheaters Club. The letter stated that he had been nominated by a fellow member who had heard of his exploits and considered him to be worthy of membership.

At first, Leo was cautious, but his curiosity got the best of him, so he made the choice to participate in the club's upcoming meeting, taking place in a dimly lit basement, unknown to outsiders. The club members divulged their dishonest exploits, striving to surpass one another in audacity and ingenuity. As they recounted their tales, they frequently burst into laughter, reveling in the misfortunes of their unsuspecting victims.

As the night wore on, Leo found himself becoming more and more addicted to the tales of infidelity and deception. He even began to share some of his own experiences, earning him a round of applause from his newfound brothers in deceit.

However, his joy was short-lived. As he was leaving the club, he was confronted by the police, who had been tipped off about the meeting by an anonymous source. It turned out that the club was actually a front for a group of undercover private investigators trying to catch cheating spouses in the act of revealing what they had done.

Caught red-handed, Greg was arrested, charged, and convicted on multiple counts of infidelity and larceny. He spent the next 16 months in prison, where he had plenty of time to reflect on his actions and the consequences they had inflicted.

In the end, Leo emerged from prison a changed man. He dissolved his membership in The Cheaters Club and vowed to never cheat again, not even on his taxes. From that day forward, he dedicated himself to living a life of honesty and fidelity. He even started a support group for reformed cheaters called "Cheaters Anonymous."

However, as time passed, Leo's reputation as a reformed cheater began to fade, and he found himself yearning for the excitement and thrill of his former life. One day, he stumbled upon a social media platform that promised to connect him with like-minded individuals who shared his passion for secret affairs.

Eager to indulge in his desires once more, he created a profile and began to scour the platform, planting seeds of seduction for potential playmates. He carefully crafted his messages, using wit and charm to entice his targets into his web of lust.

Before long, Leo had amassed a small "harem" of women who were all too eager to engage in his sordid activities. He reveled in his newfound success, believing that he had finally found a way to have his cake and eat it, too, and not get caught.

But, as with all good things, Leo's run of luck eventually came to an end. One of the women he had been seeing, a seductive but vengeful woman by the name of Vanessa, had grown tired of sharing him with his other conquests.

Determined to bring his cheating ways to an end, Vanessa hatched a plan. She created a fake profile on the same social media platform and began to chat with Leo, posing as an attractive and available woman looking for some excitement in her life. As the two began to exchange messages, Vanessa carefully crafted a trap for him. She convinced him to meet her at a local hotel, promising him a night of kinky passion and adventure that he would never forget.

Unbeknownst to Leo, Vanessa had enlisted the help of a private investigator, who had been documenting his every move, systematically gathering evidence since she discovered his game. As he entered the hotel room, Leo was greeted by a team of police officers, who promptly arrested him.

The news of his arrest quickly spread through the town, and his reputation was once again in tatters. As he sat in his jail cell, Leo couldn't help but wonder if it had all been worth it.

In the end, he learned the hard way that the allure of a secret life of infidelity wasn't worth the cost of the consequences that came with it. He spent the next seven years of his life in prison, reflecting on his mistakes and vowing to never again let his desires lead him down the path of deception.

Upon learning of Leo's escapades and the consequences he faced, Lisa couldn't help but feel a sense of relief wash over her. "A leopard never changes its spots," she mused. "Thank God I managed to avoid that disaster."

Leo and his misadventures serves as a cautionary tale for anyone who might be tempted to stray from the path of honor and doing the right thing. Remember, kids – cheaters never prosper.

BETWEEN YESTERDAY AND TOMORROW

REGINA ARNOLD

BRIGHT EYES, RUSTY, & SOLDIER BOY

Old man Hobbs loved his family more than anything. Even more than his old olive green '72 Chevy pickup. Even more than his backyard garden, where he grew several varieties of vegetables and flowers for his wife of 39 years. He still referred to her as his bride. And she still blushed when he did.

But if you didn't know him, you'd think he was just some ornery old guy who loved to tell stories about his days as a riverboat captain on the Mississippi Delta Queen. His favorite one was the time one of the passengers got drunk on champagne and puked all over another passenger's shoes. If he said, "Those were the days" once, he must have said it a few hundred times. His bride, Josie, would shake her head, roll her eyes, and tease him saying, "Hon, you've told that story so many times, we all know it word for word."

Their son, Gary, chimed in, "Yea, Pop, would you mind putting a lid on it at dinner tonight? Anna and her kids are looking forward to meeting you and Mom, so it would be cool if you'd try not to dominate the conversation."

"OK, son, I'll try to behave myself," he chuckled. "But if she's as good lookin' as you say she is, I might flirt with her a little." Josie gave him that 'look' saying, "Hobbs, you're incorrigible!"

Gary met Anna when she came into his mortgage company to sign the documents for the house she had just purchased for her and the kids, Ashley and Phillip. She was a graceful, beautiful woman, her honey blonde hair scooped up into a bun with tendrils draping her slender neck. And during the signing, it was all he could do to keep from staring at her eyes – a mesmerizing shade of crystal blue, like the depths of a calm ocean on a clear day. They seemed to hold the secrets of the universe within their sparkling depths, drawing him in with their captivating allure.

He knew he had to make his move before she left his office, so with his charming southern accent, he asked if she'd be interested in joining him for dinner some time, and was pleasantly surprised when she agreed. They dated for six weeks, having fun getting to know each other, and now their courtship was about to be strengthened by an evening with her kids, Ashley and Phillip, Josie, and Hobbs, marking the beginning of a new chapter in their relationship.

Anna's heart fluttered with excitement as she and the kids arrived for dinner. She sensed a sort of mystery in the air, a feeling that something unexpected was about to happen. She couldn't quite put her finger on what it was, but the anticipation was as thrilling as a secret shared with a close friend.

As they settled into their seats, the kids' laughter filled the room, adding a joyful soundtrack to the evening. Even the dim light of the dining room table candles cast playful shadows on the walls. Anna couldn't help but smile, her nerves replaced by a sense of adventure. Whatever the evening had in store, she was ready to enjoy it.

Hobbs loved to make cornbread from scratch, and Josie had been cooking her signature red beans and rice all afternoon, a family recipe passed down through generations of southern women. Anna complimented Josie and Hobbs on their culinary skills. They both laughed and said they were secret recipes, never to be revealed, except if someone politely asked. Anna was enamored with their sense of humor, hospitality, and the feeling that she had just come home. Way different than how she felt at her own mom and step dad's house.

Then Hobbs looked at her intensely and asked, "Where'd you get those eyes, darlin? From your daddy or your mama?"

"My dad. Mom's eyes are brown. Dad passed away several years ago and I didn't really get to know him. They were divorced when I was young." Then she stopped, wondering why she had felt so free to share that kind of information.

"I'm sorry for your loss, Bright Eyes. He missed out on a diamond in a world of rhinestones." Hobbs had a habit of giving everyone he liked a nickname, usually an endearing one. Anna felt the tears forming and a lump in her throat as she got up from her seat and hugged him, whispering, "Thank you."

He then turned to Phillip and asked, "So, Phillip, what are you planning on doing with your future?"

"I'm joining the Army when I graduate next spring. My grandfather retired as a Lieutenant Colonel and I want to carry on his legacy. He was killed in a car accident when I was two weeks old, so I never knew him, except for what Mom and Dad told me." Hobbs was stunned, almost speechless, at Phillip's determination and felt a swell of pride for this young man he had just met.

"Well, Soldier Boy, you know your mama's gonna worry about you, so are you sure about this?"

Anna felt like he was reading her mind, as she was not happy with Phillip's decision, but she also knew that it would be good for him to experience the structure and self-discipline that the Army would provide.

"Yes, sir, I'm positive. It's something I really want to do," Phillip replied.

Josie chimed in, saying, "You know, Phillip, Gary was in the Marine Corps and I'm sure he'll be able to give you some tips about what life is like in the military, especially boot camp." Gary nodded in agreement. What nobody said was that Gary was the radio operator for his platoon and his men were blown up outside of Da Nang. He suffered from survivor's guilt and never wanted to talk about it.

Hobbs quickly shifted his attention to Ashley asking, "Where did you get that red hair and those freckles, Rusty?" She blushed and giggled, answering, "From my grandma on my dad's side. She was from England and told me that the red hair in the family always skipped a generation, so I was the lucky one. I don't like my freckles, though."

They all laughed and Josie spoke up, "Aww, child, they're kisses from the sun. You're blessed."

As the conversations continued, Anna squeezed Gary's hand under the table, letting him know that she was grateful for being welcomed into his loving family. Their relationship blossomed to the point of Gary feeling comfortable enough to confide in her about his PTSD.

And every time Hobbs and Josie made red beans and rice with homemade cornbread, Bright Eyes, Rusty, and Soldier Boy were included.

SISTER'S FEATHER SONG

In the quiet of the morning,
    A girl, whose heart was hurting,
    Went out into the garden,
    Her mind riddled with questions.
    As she roamed, deep in thought,
    A vision seized her gaze,
    A solitary black feather,
    In the dew, shimmering, it laid.
    Her brother, once so lively,
    Gone too soon, now to thrive,
    In the afterlife, so silently,
    He left her this message, so timely.
    The feather, dark yet fragile,
    A symbol of his love, a token,
    Of his presence, always near,
    Though in body, he's no longer here.
    With a heart filled with gratitude,
    She held the feather, so delicate,
    Her brother's spirit, she knew,
    Was still watching, so true.
    Now, with a lightened heart,
    And a love that won't depart,
    She walks with newfound grace,

BETWEEN YESTERDAY AND TOMORROW

Her brother's memory, a sacred space.

THE BOYS

As a young child, Emily had a group of imaginary friends that she called 'the boys.' Her parents didn't discourage her, knowing that children in their early years are still close to the heavenly realms and aware of their guardian angels. But as Emily grew up, she stopped talking about them, which her parents thought was also normal.

Now, at the age of 33, Emily had a rather stressful job as the police dispatcher In the small town of Willow Creek. Hiking the picturesque trails after work often helped her unwind. She loved nature and was a kind, gentle, and beautiful soul, with a heart full of love and compassion. On the whole, her life outside of work was fairly ordinary, with a small circle of good friends.

One day Emily's life took an unexpected turn when she met a man named Dean. He was new to town, charming, handsome, and full of promise. They fell in love, and for a while, it seemed like they were destined to be together forever.

However, as time progressed, she discovered that Dean had a dark side. He was possessive, manipulative, controlling, and made promises he had no intention of keeping. Emily loved to read and each time she brought out a book, he would start some kind of argument, and then gaslight her, making her feel as though it was her fault that he wasn't getting enough of her attention. Other times he would use little niggles, irritations, and slights to take up her time and energy.

Emily knew she had gotten involved with him too quickly and that their relationship had no stable foundation. In retrospect, she wished she had run a background check on him. She couldn't take it anymore and decided to walk away, packing up and leaving one day while he was at work. Something told her that if she did it while he was home, there would be hell to pay. Just the thought of it gave her ominous chills. When Dean discovered she was gone, he was furious and felt betrayed. He wanted to make her pay for leaving him.

What Emily didn't know was that Dean already had an ultimate scheme in his twisted mind since they first met. One evening while she had been reading, he snuck into her desk and snatched her social security card. He would take out a life insurance policy on Emily, making himself the sole beneficiary. Then, he would orchestrate her death, making it look like an accident, and collect the insurance money.

Dean carefully plotted his scheme, studying Emily's daily routine and finding the perfect opportunity to execute his plan. He chose a secluded hiking trail that she used often in the nearby forest where he could stage the fatal accident.

Unbeknownst to Dean, Emily had a powerful force watching over her: the 'boys' – her designated band of guardian angels. They had been assigned to protect her from harm and guide her through life's challenges.

On the day of the planned accident, Emily felt a strange urge to go for a hike on the trail near the cliffs, the one with a spectacular view of the valley. Even though she was tired after a long day, she decided to follow her intuition anyway, and set off on the trail, unaware of the danger that was waiting for her.

Dean, lying in wait, saw Emily approaching and prepared to carry out his deadly plan. But as he made his move, the 'boys' intervened. They used their divine powers to create a distraction. A red fox darted out of the woods, heading straight for Dean. He jumped out of the way, lost his footing and fell over the cliff.

Emily, oblivious to the danger she had just escaped, continued her hike, feeling a sense of peace and gratitude for the beautiful day. Meanwhile, Dean lay injured at the bottom of the cliff, his evil plan destroyed.

As he struggled to survive, he was discovered by a group of hikers who called for help. He was taken to the hospital, where he was interrogated by the police about the contents of his backpack, and other suspicious circumstances surrounding his fall. The police interrogated Dean relentlessly until he finally confessed. Dean was arrested for attempted murder and insurance fraud.

Emily, now keenly aware of her guardian angels' protection, continued to live her life with a newfound appreciation for the beauty and safety that surrounded her, realizing that no matter what happens in life, there will always be justice and healing.

EARTH SCHOOL DROPOUT

Nigel was a peculiar little fella. Fully grown, he was only 5'2", skinny as a fence board, and bald as a bowling ball. He was all too aware of his physical shortcomings, so he constantly tried to prove himself in other ways.

On the inside, he thought of himself as an 'earth school dropout.' He always struggled with the subjects taught in earth school, such as the law of cause and effect, the law of attraction, and the law of vibration. No matter how hard he tried, Nigel just couldn't seem to grasp these concepts.

One day, Nigel decided that enough was enough. He couldn't go on living his life this way any longer. He needed to find a tutor, someone who could help him understand the mysteries of the universe and all its wonders, knowing deep down that understanding them would help him improve his life.

Nigel began his search for a tutor by asking his friends and neighbors. He approached Mr. Whiskers, the wise old cat who lived next door, hoping that he might have some insight into the workings of the universe. Mr. Whiskers, however, was more interested in napping and chasing butterflies than discussing the finer points of universal science.

Undaunted, Nigel continued his search. He asked Mrs. Hummingbird, who spent her days flitting from flower to flower, sipping nectar. Surely, she must know something about the law of cause and effect, right? Alas, Mrs. Hummingbird was too busy with her daily quest for food to provide any tutoring services.

Nigel's search for a tutor led him to some truly bizarre characters. He consulted with a group of fireflies who claimed to have a deep understanding of the cosmos, only to find that they were more interested in putting on a light show than discussing the intricacies of universal laws.

Alas, Nigel was becoming frustrated, so he decided to take a break from his search for a tutor and enjoy a quiet evening at home. As he sat in his living room, he noticed something peculiar. The lamp on his end table seemed to be casting a rather unusual shadow on the wall. Intrigued, Nigel decided to investigate.

Upon closer inspection, Nigel realized that the shadow was not a mere trick of the light. It was, in fact, an earth school teacher who had been trapped in the lamp for centuries. The teacher, a kindly old man named Mr. Shadow, had been waiting for someone to release him from his prison so he could continue his life's work of educating others.

Overjoyed at his discovery, Nigel released Mr. Shadow from the lamp, and the two quickly became good friends. Mr. Shadow agreed to tutor Nigel in the ways of earth schooling, and together, they embarked on a journey of learning and discovery.

Under Mr. Shadow's teaching, Nigel finally began to understand the complexities of the universe. He learned about the law of cause and effect – what you give out is what you get back, amplified; the law of attraction – how he could only attract experiences that aligned with his thoughts and emotions, and the law of vibration – how the energy he emitted could affect his surroundings.

While he was absorbing this information, he even discovered a few things about himself along the way. One of which was his physical appearance and how he needed to change what he thought about himself. Mr. Shadow instructed him to see himself as a whole, perfect being, loved by his Creator, no matter what he looked like to others.

In the end, Nigel realized that he didn't have to be an earth school dropout after all. With help from his friend Mr. Shadow, he had found a way to embrace who he was and become a true student of the universe.

The lesson of Nigel's story is clear: sometimes, the answers we seek are right in front of us, waiting to be discovered. We need only open our eyes and our hearts to the possibilities that surround us, and we might just find the help and guidance we've been searching for all along.

THE CHICKEN WHISPERER

What began as an effort to add a new dimension of companionship to her aging father's life, Denise decided to get a couple of chickens. Dad raised an eyebrow at first because they already had two dogs and three goats. Now she wanted to add chickens to the mix? Even though Dad remarked that they were hardly companion animals by most standards, he finally agreed.

The first two, Lucy and Ethel, became a part of the family, changing things for Dad. According to Denise, just their names made him smile.

It wasn't long before Olive, Blue, and Knickers were added to the brood. And Dad always had a say in naming them. He also made it very clear there would be no roosters. The consensus from Dad and Denise's brother was that a rooster would be way too chaotic for the three-acre family farm.

Word spread quickly through friends and social media about the flavorful, organic eggs that their free-range hens were producing. Not a lot to begin with, but enough to attract a handful of returning customers. The family farm soon became Happy Hens Haven.

Soon after that, she began to be contacted about rescuing hens from places around the entire county, where the owners could no longer take care of them. One in particular was a batch of five, who had lived their entire lives confined in a chicken tractor and were never free. Denise instinctively knew they had to be rescued and she was the one to do it.

Then came three older hens rescued from a woman who said they were mean and not laying. It didn't take Denise long to integrate them into the brood. They began laying like clockwork and getting along well with the rest of the 'ladies.' Hearing how she did it was the reason her new title spread like wildfire. She became known as the "Chicken Whisperer."

But she didn't stop there. The brood kept enlarging. Next was a group of 15 that she rescued from a man who was moving and couldn't take them with him. But the farm truck wasn't running, so she had to figure out how to get that many hens transported to the farm. She ended up putting them all in dog crates and carriers. It was like a jigsaw puzzle arranging them in her four-door passenger car, but her determination made it happen.

Eventually the count increased to 36 and Dad was proud of his enterprising daughter. Many times he would overhear her talking to egg customers, explaining what hens do when laying their eggs. She called it their little signature song, a distinctive sound each one makes as they expel the egg. He found himself grinning from ear to ear.

And then she would explain that, because of the 'bloom,' unwashed eggs can be stored for up to six weeks on the counter. She also added that most people don't like looking at them dirty, so they can be washed and refrigerated, keeping up to three weeks. She had learned so much and was always willing to educate her customers, which kept them coming back for more.

As time wore on, Dad's health took a turn for the worse, and eventually, he left this world. However, the many months of laughter and happiness that Denise and the hens brought him will forever remain among her most cherished memories. In the face of such love, no sacrifice is too great.

DEVON MEETS CARL

Devon always thought of himself as a complete catch. His income was in the mid six figures, affording him the lifestyle of a luxury flat in downtown Boston, and a Mercedes Benz convertible. However, building and maintaining successful relationships was always a struggle after the honeymoon phase wore off. Each time he began a new dating cycle, he thought, "Maybe this time it'll be different. Maybe she won't leave me." After the last one, though, who turned out to be a 100% gold-digger, he realized it was time to put his ego aside and seek some help.

During a conversation with his buddy, Marty, Devon asked, "How is it that your marriage to Peggy has lasted so long?" Marty answered with two words, "Self-awareness." He went on to explain that he, like Devon, kept repeating the same cycle of unrequited love and knew something had to change. That's when he went looking for answers.

He asked, "Have you ever heard of Carl Jung?" Devon shook his head no. "Well, he was a Swiss psychologist who founded analytical psychology, exploring the human psyche, the unconscious mind that drives all of us without us being aware of it. Maybe you should look into what he discovered. It might help you."

"Sounds pretty woo-woo to me, buddy. Not sure I want to go there, but I know you're smart, so I'll at least check it out." Devon politely thanked him and went home, thinking that it would be too much of a hassle and brushed it off. However, after his next relationship failed like the others, something told him it was time to check out Carl Jung's work. He did some extensive research online to find a starting place.

That's when he discovered Jung's book called "The Practice of Psychotherapy," which discussed the role of the unconscious mind in healing. And, being tired of the pain, Devon desperately wanted to heal. The way he looked at it, if he didn't find a way to heal himself, to become more self-aware, he would always be alone and unfulfilled, attracting partners that were also unhealed. And all of his failed romantic relationships had thoroughly exhausted him.

During his exploration, he learned that below the surface, there's a vast, uncharted territory of thoughts, emotions, and desires that he had suppressed from the world and often himself. According to what Jung said, our conscious minds are only the tip of the iceberg and that when we begin the journey of self-discovery, we're often met with a realization that can be both liberating and unsettling. Devon was already feeling unsettled but kept reading, looking for answers.

He found himself nodding in agreement with the part about how our darkest fears, desires, and impulses live in the unseen realm, our shadow side. It was a light-bulb moment for Devon when he understood that he had, like most people, been conditioned to reject, hide, or deny these feelings, fearing judgment, or being seen as a social outcast.

BETWEEN YESTERDAY AND TOMORROW

Devon's desire to make his life work better kept him up late every night, delving into the concepts of Jung's teachings. He didn't watch TV, play video games, or mindlessly scroll through social media. He was determined to create a more fulfilling life, one with real love. He wanted to break free from societal expectations, worrying about what other people thought of him, so that he could develop more authentic, honest relationships.

For a while, he went into the 'beating himself up for past mistakes' phase, making a list of the things he had kept hidden from the women in his past relationships – hidden patterns, childhood wounds, and destructive habits.

Once he did that, he revisited his list daily, confronting his shadows, until he finally reached a place of liberation, empowerment and wholeness, knowing that he could make better, more conscious choices. His transformation had begun in earnest with the realization that the light and the dark are two sides of the human condition.

One evening, sipping a glass of brandy while thinking about what he had learned, he decided to call his buddy. When Marty answered, he said, "This trip into the shadows isn't for the faint of heart, is it?"

Amused, Marty replied, "No, it certainly isn't. There's always uncertainty, but fear not, brother, in the end, it's your determination and resilience that will get you to your destination. Maybe even the love of your life."

RUMORS

In 1939, Blue Rapids was a small, rural town with a population of 842, where everyone knew each other's name and made it their business to know what everyone else was doing. Mostly farmers and their wives, who formed clubs and cliques. Because of that, rumors had a way of spreading like wildfire.

One day, Benny discovered that he had become the center of a gossip storm, an assault on his character. Something he never would have imagined.

Benny was always a genuine, kind-hearted, and hardworking young man, admired by many for his strong work ethic and unwavering dedication to his family's business, Langford Dairy. However, one day, a malicious rumor began to circulate through the community, insinuating that he was stealing from the dairy.

As the gossip intensified, Benny's once-friendly neighbors began to cast judgmental side glances his way, and whispers followed him everywhere he went. Despite his innocence, the rumor continued to grow, fueled by the town's inclination to gossip.

His once-peaceful life began to crumble around him, as Langford Dairy experienced a sharp decline in business. Customers, once loyal patrons, now avoided the dairy, fearing that they might be supporting a thief. Benny was horrified, not knowing what to do. Realizing that the odds were against him, but determined to clear his name and save the family's business, he had no choice but to launch his own investigation into the matter. With the help of his childhood friend, Tom, he began to unravel the truth behind the malicious rumor.

As Benny and Tom dug deeper into the mystery, they discovered that the rumor had been started by a disgruntled former bookkeeper, who had been fired by Benny's father, Francis, for pocketing cash payments from the dairy's customers. This employee, Marjorie, seeking revenge, had made up the story about Benny to cover up her crime and get even with Francis for letting her go.

Benny, Tom, and Francis went to Marjorie's house to confront her, just as she was packing up her old Model T to leave town. The guys didn't have to say a word. She knew she was guilty and it had been eating at her, but she was afraid of the consequences, so she thought running was the best solution. Eventually, she confessed to her scheme and was arrested. With the truth now out in the open, the town's people began to see Benny in a new light, and his reputation was restored.

His determination to uncover the truth and clear his name not only saved the dairy, but also brought the community of Blue Rapids closer together. The experience shed a rather bright light on the power of gossip and the importance of finding the truth before casting judgment on others.

LIFE BEFORE THE INTERNET

Jill and her mother were shopping one day, leisurely looking through the aisles for some kitchen utensils for her new apartment. She had just graduated from college, landed a good job, and was now independent, but still loved spending time with her mom.

Jill noticed a toddler, two years old at most, watching a video on his mother's cell phone. His mom wasn't paying attention to him and apparently gave him her phone to keep him occupied while she shopped.

When Jill and her mom got back to her place, she sat at the kitchen table, thinking about that kid in the cart and asked her mom a question, "Hey Mom, what was life like before the internet?"

"Why do you want to know, Jillie?"

"Just curious. That little boy I saw today with his mom's phone made me wonder."

Her mom smiled, knowing that what she was about to say was going to become a teaching moment.

"Well, dear daughter, let me share what it was like. In a world before the internet, life was a different experience altogether. Everyone called people instead of texting. They used corded phones, sometimes with a 50 foot curly cord so they could still see what the kids were doing while they were on the phone. They wrote handwritten cards, thank you notes, and letters instead of emails. There was no Google, so kids got together in study groups and rode their bikes to the library to look things up. People visited their grandparents in person as often as possible, instead of video calling. They engaged in conversation with grocery store clerks instead of pushing buttons on a screen at self-checkout kiosks. They were more respectful of differing opinions on important issues, even politics and religion, because they couldn't hide behind a keyboard. Writers typed their manuscripts on typewriters instead of computer screens. People kept handwritten journals and diaries, often with a lock and key. They experienced the joy and smell of holding a brand new paper book in their hands. They looked into each other's eyes and had conversations around the dinner table instead of burying their faces in their phones. They played board games, watched movies together, and ate fresh popcorn. They experienced real life camaraderie, gathered in coffee shops, mom and pop diners, at church potlucks, and picnics in the park on pleasant Sunday afternoons. They spent more time in nature up close instead of looking at travel websites of places that they would never be able to see in person. They drove cars that didn't have internal computers. The kids would often wake up early to catch their favorite Saturday morning cartoons on TV. After breakfast, it was common for them to meet up with their friends to play outside or go to the park and enjoy the swings and monkey bars. They would spend hours reading books, drawing, coloring, or learning to play a musical instrument. These activities not only provided them with a sense of accomplishment but also helped to develop their creativity and imagination."

Jill was silent, soaking it all in, detail by detail. Her mom had painted a vivid picture of life before the internet as a time of innocence, beauty, and simplicity. She made a vow to slow down her pace and connect more deeply with other people, especially those she loved.

"Thanks, Mom. It sounds like it was wonderful! Do you ever wish that life was still like that?"

"I think just about everyone in my generation does. The current world moves way too fast and the simplicity of those times seems to be lost."

"You know what, Mom? I want kids someday and I'm gonna make darn sure they grow up knowing some of the simple pleasures of days gone by before the internet."

THREE MOMS & A PIE

Once upon a time, in the heart of a sleepy town called Grainger, there was a horseshoe-shaped street known as Rose Circle. It was a place where houses with well-groomed lawns and blooming rose gardens stood proudly, and children played safely in the streets. Little did the residents know that their lives were about to change when three divorced moms moved into the community.

Susan moved in first, a hardworking single mother of two, striving to provide the best life possible for her children. She had a sharp wit and a no-nonsense attitude, which often concealed her insecurities.

Then there was Karen, a kind-hearted woman with a love for baking, who had a son and a daughter. Her divorce had left her emotionally drained, but she was determined to rebuild her life. Lastly, there was Linda, a free-spirited soul with an infectious laugh and two teenage daughters. She had been a housewife all her life and was now learning to navigate the world as a single mom.

As the three women settled into their new homes, they quickly discovered that life in Rose Circle wasn't as ideal as it seemed. The community was tight-knit, and the neighbors began to talk. Susan, Karen, and Linda were the latest hot topic, and their struggles to make ends meet were no secret.

Despite the prying eyes and chattering busy bodies, the three women found comfort in each other. They shared their stories, their fears, and their dreams over cups of coffee and slices of Karen's signature lemon meringue pie. As their friendship blossomed, they began to pool their resources, having each other's backs when times got tough.

One particularly difficult time, when there was more month than money, Susan, Karen, and Linda decided to put their heads together and create a plan. Susan, with her business background, suggested they start their own small business. Karen, with her baking skills, could provide the goods, while Linda, with her creativity, could design the marketing materials. Together, they launched "Three Moms and a Pie," a home-based bakery that quickly became a local favorite. So much that they had to find space to rent and buy some equipment, but, using their profits, they did it.

As their business thrived, so did their friendship. They supported each other through thick and thin, celebrating successes and comforting each other during hardships. The once-gossipy neighbors began to see the strength and resilience of the trio, and slowly, they, too, were welcomed into the Rose Circle community.

Years passed, and their children grew. Susan's two kids became successful professionals, one in health care and the other in engineering. Karen's son pursued his passion for music, while her daughter went to nursing school, and Linda's daughters made names for themselves in the graphic design world. Despite their busy lives, the three moms remained close, always finding time to catch up over coffee and pie.

One afternoon, as they reflected on their memorable journey, Susan asked, "Do you guys remember the dinners of hot dogs and beans back in the old days when money was scarce and we had to cash in empty soda bottles? And that old '63 Ford I had with the bumper sticker that read, "Don't Honk, I'm Pedaling as Fast as I Can?" Laughing, the other two nodded their heads. Linda mused, "Those were the days that made us who we are, ladies. We gave it all we had, didn't we?"

At that moment, they all realized that their struggles and triumphs had made them stronger, both individually and as a blended family. They created a life that was far from perfect, but it was a life filled with love, laughter, and the unbreakable bond of friendship.

And so, as the sun set on Rose Circle that evening, the three divorced moms looked back on their time there together, knowing that it was the most profound growth period of their lives. For they had learned that sometimes, it's in the darkest moments that the brightest stars are born, and the power of friendship can overcome even the greatest challenges.

THE JANITOR

In the heart of the bustling city of Samara, there stood a magnificent museum that housed countless treasures and artifacts from around the world. Among these priceless relics was the Celestial Crown, an ancient headdress adorned with glittering jewels. According to legend, it was said to be worn by a high priestess who possessed mystical powers. It was the museum's most valuable artifact and the pride of the city.

One day, a young and clumsy janitor named Sergei was assigned to clean the museum's exhibits. He was a kind-hearted soul, but was prone to unexpected accidents, which is why, most of the time, he was assigned only to mopping and polishing the marble floors.

But today, as he dusted the glass display case containing the Celestial Crown, his elbow nudged the case's latch, causing it to swing open. In a panic, he reached out to catch the falling artifact but accidentally knocked it off its pedestal.

The Celestial Crown tumbled to the ground, shattering into tiny pieces. Sergei froze and stared in horror at the wreckage, realizing the gravity of what had just happened. He couldn't believe his eyes, but knew he'd have to confess to the museum's curator, Mr. Popov.

Sergei went to his office and, in a shaky voice, he confessed. "Mr. Popov, I, uh, uh, I have terrible news. I accidentally broke the Celestial Crown."

Mr. Popov's face turned pale as he rushed to the scene. Upon seeing the shattered artifact, he let out a deep sigh.

"Oh, Sergei, how could you be so careless? This artifact was priceless! It cannot be replaced."

Sergei, filled with guilt and remorse, offered to do anything to make amends.

"I'll do whatever it takes to fix this, Sir. I'll pay for the repairs, work overtime, anything!"

Moved by his sincerity, Mr. Popov decided to give him a chance to redeem himself. He tasked him with finding a way to restore the Celestial Crown, no matter the cost.

Over the next few weeks, Sergei relentlessly set out on a quest to find a solution. He searched out experts in ancient artifacts, historians, and even consulted with a renowned alchemist, Professor Vasiliev. After much research and persistence, Sergei discovered an ancient scroll that contained the secret to restoring broken artifacts.

In his excitement, Sergei stuttered but finally got the words out, "Professor Vasiliev, the gods must be smiling on us. I've found the answer! This scroll contains the formula to restore the Celestial Crown!"

"Well done! But be warned, the process is dangerous and requires great skill. Are you sure you're prepared for this?"

Sergei, determined to make things right, agreed to undertake the perilous task. With the help of the Professor, he carefully followed the ancient instructions, combining rare ingredients and performing intricate tasks of piecing it together so the seams wouldn't be visible.

After weeks of intensely hard work, and a miracle from the heavenly realms, the restoration process was complete. The Celestial Crown, once shattered and lifeless, now glowed with renewed brilliance. The mystical artifact had been restored to its former glory.

Sergei presented the restored crown to Mr. Popov, who was astonished by the miraculous recovery.

"I'm so relieved. You've done the impossible! You not only saved the museum's most valuable treasure but also preserved the city's pride. I'm proud of you, my boy."

When word got out about what happened, Sergei was no longer known as the clumsy janitor. He was celebrated as the hero who saved the Celestial Crown, a symbol of hope and resilience in the face of disaster.

Sergei's learning experience, as frustrating as it was, increased his confidence as he enjoyed the spotlight. Yet, he continued his studies with the Professor as his mentor, eager to uncover further mysteries concealed within the ancient scrolls. He was no longer referred to as the clumsy janitor.

LOCKED ROOMS

In the mansion of life, we tread with care,
Through countless rooms, but some remain bare,
Behind closed doors, secrets are kept,
Of thoughts and fears, memories adept.
We wander halls, our minds in a haze,
Each step we take, in life's endless maze,
But locked doors taunt, their secrets concealed,
A mystery that none of us revealed.
In these chambers, what do we find?
Regrets and worries, left behind,
The key to unlock, we hold in our hand,
Yet fear and doubt make us understand,
That locked doors, once opened, may show,
The shadows we've long tried to forgo,
And so we tread, with hearts full of dread,
Afraid to face the truths unsaid.
But life's a journey, and we must learn,
To face our fears, and secrets overturn,
For in the locked rooms, we may find,
The courage to leave our fears behind.

WHEN FAERIES GO ROGUE

Nestled in the heart of the hidden woods, between towering weeping willows and crystal clear streams, was the charming village of Whisperwood, always teeming with the laughter of tiny, winged creatures known as faeries. These magical beings, adorned in vibrant colors and shimmering wings, were known throughout the woods for their playful antics. They reveled in the joy of life, spreading happiness and wonder wherever they went.

However, most of the humans living in Whisperwood were unable to see these mysterious creatures because the faeries existed in a higher, harmonious vibration. On certain occasions, when children were playing in the woods, they would giggle with delight as the faeries made themselves visible. When their mothers asked why they were so excited, their reply was, "Can't you see them, Mother?" Alas, the mothers were never able to catch even a glimpse.

The village was ruled by the wise and divine Queen Magnolia, whose beauty was surpassed only by her wisdom. Under her reign, the faeries lived in harmony, their days filled with laughter, music, and dance. However, even in the most harmonious settings, trouble can brew beneath the surface.

One fateful day, a group of young, restless faeries, led by their rambunctious ring leader, Mirthwhistle, grew bored with their simple lives. They yearned for adventure, excitement, and the thrill of untamed shenanigans. They plotted in secret, hatching a plan to break free from the confines of their territory and take a journey through other villages in the woods.

As the sun dipped below the horizon, casting a warm glow over the terrain, the rogue faeries took flight, leaving behind their bewildered friends and family. They soared through the air, their laughter echoing through the treetops, as they reveled in their newfound freedom. The hidden woods, however, was not prepared for the whirlwind of mischief that was about to be unleashed.

The first stop on their journey was the neighboring village of pixies. The rogue faeries descended upon the unsuspecting pixies, causing havoc in their once peaceful lives. They swapped hats, mixed up potions, and hid the village's most prized possessions under rocks and clover beds. The bewildered pixies scurried about, trying to make sense of the chaos that had just invaded their realm.

The rogue faeries, now fueled by the thrill of their escapades, continued their journey, leaving a trail of echoed confusion in their wake. They ventured into the realm of the gnomes, where they played pranks on the hardworking creatures, turning their meticulously tended gardens into wild jungles and their perfectly crafted tools into twisted, unrecognizable shapes.

As news of the rogue faeries' antics spread, the inhabitants of the hidden forest began to fear for their safety. The wise Queen, saddened by the pranks of her subjects, knew that she must act quickly to bring them back to their senses.

She summoned her most trusted advisors and devised a plan to track down the rogue faeries and restore order to the realm. The Queen and her entourage set out on their journey, following the trail of mischief that Mirthwhistle and the rogues had left behind.

As they traveled deeper into the heart of the forest, they encountered the victims of the rogue faeries, who shared tales of their misfortunes and pointed the way to the culprits. The Queen's resolve to find her wayward subjects only grew stronger with each encounter, and her determination to bring them back to their village never wavered.

Finally, after many days of travel, the Queen and her companions stumbled upon the rogue faeries, who were in the midst of wreaking havoc upon the home of the unicorns. The majestic creatures, their once pristine manes and tails now tangled and knotted, looked on in despair as their sanctuary was reduced to chaos. One of the bewildered unicorns, Rona, was covered in sticky, glittery faerie dust from ears to tail.

The Queen, heartbroken by the sight before her, confronted the faeries, her voice filled with both love and disappointment. She chided them, saying, "Let me remind you of the joy and harmony you once shared in our village and the importance of your roles as protectors of the hidden forest. I will forgive you on one condition – you must personally apologize to every creature you've harmed." The rogue faeries, their faces stained with tears, listened intently to the Queen's words, their hearts heavy with the weight of what they had done.

In that moment, they unanimously realized the error of their ways and the true value of the life they had left behind.

"Your Majesty, you have my word that we won't do anything like this again and we will apologize to all," Mirthwhistle responded. They all begged for the Queen's forgiveness, promising to return to their village and dedicate themselves to the betterment of their community.

The compassionate Queen, her heart swelling with love, welcomed the rogue faeries back into her embrace, forgiving them for their transgressions. Together, they returned to their village, where they were greeted with open arms and the promise of a brighter future.

In the years that followed, the hidden forest flourished once again, its inhabitants working together to create a world filled with laughter, love, and the magic of friendship. The rogue faeries, now reformed, became some of the most dedicated and loyal members of their community, their previous misadventures serving as a reminder of the importance of unity and the power of forgiveness.

MONK OF MACHU PICCHU

Ever since he was a kid and had read a book about how people from all over the world made pilgrimages to Machu Picchu, Antonio wanted to go on his own quest someday to explore the ancient ruins. The city, shrouded in mystery and steeped in history, offered an experience unlike any other. He scoured websites and read personal stories of those whose lives had changed after taking their journey. Fascinated and curious, he booked a two-week trip to Machu Picchu the following April.

He was determined to make this a solo pilgrimage, so he didn't participate in guided tours. As he wandered through the stone pathways and marveled at the architectural wonders of the ancient Incan civilization, it was his hope to gain a deeper understanding of himself and his place in the world .

One morning he set out early, exploring the outskirts of the ruins and stumbled upon a secluded cave. Intrigued, he ventured inside and discovered a monk meditating in the dimly lit space. The monk, draped in a scarlet robe, seemed to exude a sense of tranquility and wisdom.

Curious about the monk's presence in such an isolated location, Antonio approached him. The monk, unfazed by the sudden intrusion, calmly opened his eyes and greeted the young man with a warm smile. The two began to discuss life, the universe, and the meaning of existence.

Two hours went by as the monk shared his belief that the key to understanding oneself is through solitude. He explained that by taking some time every day to detach from the distractions and chaos of everyday life, one can go deep into their inner self and confront their fears, unmet needs, and emotions. He emphasized that true self-awareness can only be achieved by embracing quiet reflection.

Even though Antonio was initially skeptical of the monk's words, he began to ponder this idea, thoughts swirling in his mind. He realized that in his quest for success and worldly pleasures, he had often neglected his inner self and put his personal growth on the back burner. The monk's teachings resonated with him, so he decided to start practicing being alone, shutting out the world for a while, in order to discover his true identity.

Antonio extended his hand to say farewell to the wise monk. and the monk, with his warm smile, stated, "Remember, my friend, life is a journey, not a destination. Embrace the lessons of each moment and let them guide you along your path. A word of caution, though. Once you choose this path, you may find it difficult to be around certain people with chaotic minds. Believe me when I say you'll know who they are."

Antonio returned to his journey, with a newfound appreciation for solitude and self-reflection. As he continued his travels, he made a conscious effort to carve out time for quiet introspection and contemplation. With each passing day, he woke up with a growing sense of inner peace and self-awareness, ultimately leading him to a profound understanding of his purpose and place in the world.

DANGEROUS PERSON

Laney was known for her fierce independence and her ability to face life's challenges head-on. But it wasn't always that way. As a youngster, she was shy and awkward, especially around people who were outwardly dominating.

Now, as an adult, she realized that she really did possess the power of choice. Rather than reacting immediately to tough situations, she understood the necessity of taking some time to weigh all of her options before responding. When faced with adversity, she would retreat into solitude, connecting with God, only to emerge stronger than before. This was a trait that had earned her a reputation from those in her inner circle as a 'dangerous' person because they didn't understand her process.

Things were moving along well with her custom T-shirt printing business, her 'baby,' until the economy began to decline and people's buying habits changed. Laney found herself in the midst of a financial crisis, her once-thriving business now in a downward spiral. In her initial excitement to get started, she made the mistake of not factoring in the possibility of an economic downturn. Friends and family offered their support, sometimes with intriguing ideas for a short-term solution, but she knew she couldn't get sidetracked. Laney was determined to bring it back to life on her own. She thought, "I created this from scratch and made some mistakes, so it's up to me to fix them and turn it around."

As days turned into weeks, she became engrossed in her work, hardly taking time to sleep or eat. She plunged into the complexities of her business plan, collaborated with suppliers, learned lessons from her errors, and discovered novel solutions to salvage her company from devastation..

Meanwhile, her friends and family watched with concern, fearing that her relentless pursuit of independence would cause burnout and lead to her downfall. They whispered behind her back, criticizing her for daring to face her struggles alone.

She could sense that those closest to her, even though they might have meant well, were talking behind her back, but Laney remained unfazed by their judgments. She knew that her strength, resilience, and business savvy had leveled up and were her greatest assets, so she refused to let anyone dim her light. She also came to the conclusion that if she handed off the responsibility to someone else, the problem would only repeat itself down the road, because the lesson was hers, and hers alone, to learn.

Finally, after months of tireless effort, she emerged victorious. Her business not only recovered but thrived, surpassing all previous success. The once-doubtful onlookers marveled at her tenacity and admired her courage.

Laney, however, remained humble. Never once was she tempted to say, "I told you I could do it." Even though her journey had been littered with obstacles and there were times when she wanted to throw in the towel, getting back up again was a testament to her unwavering determination.

And so, the phrase "you're a dangerous person if you go through things alone and come back better" became a symbol of Laney's undaunted spirit – a reminder that true strength lies in the ability to face adversity head-on, and that independence, when combined with faith and resilience, can lead to greatness.

When you feel like throwing in the towel, God throws it back and says, "Wipe your face and get back in the ring."

I WISH WE COULD

I wish we could stay here forever,
  In a world where time stands still,
  Where the sun never sets, and the moon never wanes,
  A place where love and joy bend to our will.
  Here, where the skies are painted in hues of gold,
  And the breeze sings a melody so bold,
  In this haven, where our heart's desires are met,
  Where the soul finds solace, and sorrows forget.
  But alas! This paradise, only a dream,
  A fleeting moment, a wistful gleam,
  For life, with its transient nature, takes us away,
  And the world, with its chaos begins a new day.

BREAKING THE BOX

"She's just too different. Why can't she be like everyone else?" That's how most people saw Rebecca – different.

But she had always been different. Never liked being in large crowds, small talk, or getting involved in other people's business. The others thought she was a lone wolf, hiding some kind of secret. But there was no secret. She knew she was different, but didn't understand why that was a bad thing. It's just that she was known for her unique and unconventional ideas, her imaginative thoughts, and her free spirit. That's the reason why those around her often tried to fit her into a box that they thought was suitable for her; to be more like them.

Whenever Rebecca was facing a problem, she often took walks to clear her head. One day while in the park, she noticed an old man sitting on a bench. He reminded her of her deceased grandfather, so she decided to approach him and strike up a conversation. As she sat down on the bench beside him, he said, "Hello, Rebecca." Surprised, she asked, "How did you know my name?"

"Well, my dear, everyone around here does."

Gazing down, she said, "Yea, I guess they do."

The old man could see she was troubled and asked her what it was. She explained how everyone was trying to put her in a box. He listened intently, then spoke with a gentle smile.

"The sad truth is, Rebecca, people often fear what they don't understand. They feel threatened by anything that challenges their beliefs or the way they live their lives. That's why they try to put you in a box. It makes them feel safe and in control."

Tears welled up in her eyes as she protested, "But I don't want to be in a box! I want to be free to be myself."

"I understand, my dear," the old man replied. "But you must also understand that you can't change the way others think. What you can do, however, is break free from the box they've created for you."

"But how?" she asked, feeling a glimmer of hope.

"By honoring your uniqueness and standing up for yourself," the old man replied. "Show them that you are more than they perceive you to be. Lead by example, let your light shine, and inspire others to break free from their own boxes."

Rebecca nodded, feeling a newfound determination within her. From that day on, she started to speak up for herself and share her ideas, unconcerned about what anyone else thought. Slowly but surely, the people began to see her for who she truly was – a strong, imaginative, and inspiring young girl who was breaking free from the box that the others had tried to confine her in.

GEORGE & THE STORAGE UNIT

George and his wife, Paula, were having dinner in their new place one night when he told her what happened when he visited his old storage unit earlier that day.

"When I rolled up the door, I couldn't believe my eyes. Boxes upon boxes, furniture stacked high, and knick-knacks galore. It's been so long since I was there, and now it was overflowing with items I couldn't even remember collecting."

"Are you kidding? How long has it been?" she asked. George admitted it had been at least five years. Paula was shocked, but let him continue.

"As I began to explore all that stuff, I came across some of my most treasured possessions. There was the antique furniture I had inherited from my grandparents, each piece holding a story of its own. I remembered the times we spent together, admiring the workmanship and the history those pieces represented.

Then there were the vintage records I had collected during my college years. The Beatles, The Rolling Stones, and so many more artists whose music had shaped my youth. I could almost hear the melodies playing in my head as I held each album in my hands. It was awesome!

And way in the back, I found a series of expensive artworks that I had bought from a fairly renowned artist. Each one is a masterpiece, capturing the essence of the world around us. I had always admired his work and was proud to own a part of his legacy.

I also found a box of old photographs and documents, and as I sifted through them, I found items that belonged to my parents. When they passed away, I had inherited these items, but had never found the time to sort through them. Letters, certificates, and even old family recipes – each one brought back a precious memory of the past.

As I sat there, surrounded by the remnants of my life, I realized how much I had let go of over the years. The storage unit, once a forgotten space, now holds the key to my past and the memories I had long buried."

Paula listened as he talked on and on, a bit perplexed by everything he had rediscovered from his past.

"I have an idea. You might think it's a little far-fetched, but hear me out, honey. Let's take everything out of the storage unit and move all of your memories to that empty building down by the tack room. It's concrete block, so it will stay cool in the summer months. We could turn it into a mini museum, a place where you could showcase your collection and share the stories behind each item. I think it would be a fun way to invite people from around town to visit and experience the joy of collecting, just as you did. What do you think?"

George loved her idea and said, "Yes! That old building! What a perfect way to show people the importance of preserving the past and cherishing the memories that make us who we are."

MOSES MEETS PATIENCE

When Corrie's daughter, Melanie, was 15, she decided that she knew everything (of course, don't they all?) and didn't want to honor her curfew. Corrie thought 10:00 pm was pretty liberal, but her daughter disagreed. She was also hanging out with some older kids, whom Corrie didn't approve of and told her what she thought about her choices. Ground rules were set, but Melanie kept breaking them. That's when she decided to run away from home.

As a divorced mom, Corrie was devastated. She didn't know where Melanie had gone and who she could turn to, so she drove the streets in their town, but couldn't find her. Melanie's brother couldn't help because he was in the Army, stationed in Germany. When Corrie called Melanie's father, he said there was nothing he could do. That meant that he was unavailable as well. Lots of expletives were exchanged.

Shortly after hanging up the phone, Corrie walked out on the balcony of her home, looked down and thought, "I could jump, but I'd only hurt myself. Damn!"

That's when she was reminded of how Moses went to the burning bush. Terrified as he was to approach it, he heard the voice of God. She looked up to the heavens and said, "God, I can't do this by myself. You're gonna have to take over." Suddenly she felt like Moses.

This is where she could say that she heard God's voice, but actually she didn't hear a voice at all. It's what she *felt* that made her realize she wasn't alone. She felt a sense of peace. She imagined God saying, "Be patient. I'm taking care of both of you."

What else could Corrie do but be patient and pray? She had already exhausted all attempts to find Melanie by herself. So she went to work but didn't let anyone know what was going on. After all, she had a business to run. Later that day, Corrie got a call from a friend who casually mentioned that she ran into Melanie at the grocery store. This was her first sign that God was working on it ..."Patience, my dear, patience."

The next day when she woke up, Corrie had a strong intuitive urge to call the police and report her daughter as a runaway minor, so she did. Two days later, she received a call from a youth advocate agency. Melanie had been brought there by the police. Corrie thanked God and went to pick up her daughter, but before she was allowed to do so, she was cautioned by a counselor that Melanie was belligerent about her mother calling the police. Imagine that!

The counselor explained that all the values Corrie had taught her had gone out the window, but assured her that, at some point, they would return and to just be patient. Corrie thought, "Is that you again, God, with the patience thing?" The counselor also recommended some tough love techniques and they worked.

Did they live happily ever after? Yes and no. There were other incidents, but at least Corrie knew that, like Moses, she could always return to the burning bush for help, blessings, and necessary character-building lessons like patience.

ACTIONS SPEAK

Oliver had a peculiar quirk. Though his heart was filled with gratitude about life, he struggled to express his thanks to those around him. His words often failed him, and his attempts at showing appreciation were clumsy and awkward.

One Friday morning, as he was walking to work, he came across a little girl who had dropped her ice cream cone on the sidewalk. The girl looked heartbroken, tears streaming down her face."Are you alright?" Oliver asked, feeling a pang of sympathy for the child.

The girl sniffled and nodded, wiping her tears away. "I just wanted an ice cream, but now it's all gone," she whimpered.

Oliver's heart swelled with empathy, and he wished he could do something to make her feel better. He reached into his pocket and pulled out a crumpled dollar bill.

"Here, take this," he said, offering the girl the money. "You can buy another one."

The girl's eyes widened, but she hesitated for a second before accepting the bill. "Thank you, mister!" she exclaimed, her face lighting up with a smile.

Oliver felt a strange warmth in his chest as he watched the girl skip away, her sadness replaced with joy. He knew he had done something good and was grateful for the opportunity to help, but couldn't quite put his feelings into words.

Later that day at work, Oliver's colleague, Sarah, noticed his distant demeanor. "Is everything alright, Oliver?" she asked, concerned about him.

"I just ... I don't know how to say it," Oliver stammered, his cheeks flushing with embarrassment. "I did something nice today, and I feel good about it, but I can't express it properly.

"Sarah smiled gently. "You know, Oliver, sometimes actions speak louder than words. You don't always have to say something to show your feelings. Just being there for someone, or doing something kind can be enough."

Oliver thought about Sarah's remark as he walked home that evening. He realized that, despite his difficulty in expressing his feelings, he had managed to make a positive impact on someone's day. And perhaps that was enough.

From that day on, Oliver made a conscious effort to show his feelings through his actions. He used his spare time to help raise money for local charities, and became a bell ringer for the Salvation Army at Christmas time. Though he still struggled to find the right words, he knew that his actions spoke volumes.

And, as he continued to spread kindness and gratitude throughout his community, Oliver began to understand that expressing himself wasn't just about the words he spoke. It was about the love and compassion he shared with those around him. A language that transcended words.

THE CAMP-OUT

The Johnson family was no stranger to the occasional power outage. Living in a city with an aging electrical grid, they had become quite familiar with navigating life without electricity. But when the power went out on a warm fall evening, they decided to make the best of the situation and have a little adventure.

"Hey, kids, how about we have a camping trip in the backyard?" suggested Mr. Johnson, his eyes twinkling with excitement.

The children, Amber and Tommy, exchanged skeptical glances before breaking into wide grins. "Yay! OK! Can we tell scary stories?" Amber asked eagerly.

"Of course! And we'll build a campfire, too," Mr. Johnson replied, clearly enjoying the idea.

As the sun began to set, the Johnson family ventured into their backyard, carrying sleeping bags, blankets, flashlights, and an assortment of camping gear. Mrs. Johnson, however, was less than thrilled about the prospect of sleeping outside.

"I don't know about this, dear," she said, her voice wavering with uncertainty. "What if there are bugs? Or that annoying racoon?"

Mr. Johnson patted her hand reassuringly. "Don't worry, honey. We'll be perfectly safe. Think of it as an adventure!"

With that, the family set up their makeshift campsite, complete with a tent, a campfire, and a s'mores station. As the darkness descended, they huddled around the fire, roasting marshmallows and sharing ghost stories.

But as the night wore on, the Johnsons began to realize that backyard camping was not quite the adventure they had hoped for. Mrs. Johnson was tormented by the relentless buzzing of mosquitoes, while Amber and Tommy struggled to find a comfortable position on the lumpy ground.

To make matters worse, the campfire began to die down, leaving the family shrouded in darkness. And the weather had shifted, turning a pleasant breeze into a chilly wind. Mr. Johnson attempted to reignite the flames, but his efforts were met with no success.

"Maybe we should just go back inside," Mrs. Johnson suggested, her voice trembling with cold and exhaustion.

But Mr. Johnson was determined to see their adventure through. "No, no, we can't give up now! We'll just have to find another way to stay warm."

And so, the Johnson family huddled together under a mountain of blankets, their teeth chattering and their noses red with cold. As they drifted off to sleep, they couldn't help but wonder if perhaps they had underestimated the challenges of backyard camping.

The next morning, as the sun rose and the power was restored, the Johnson family emerged from their backyard adventure, bleary-eyed and bedraggled. But despite the hardships they had faced, they couldn't help but laugh at the absurdity of their situation.

"Well, that was certainly an adventure we won't soon forget," Mr. Johnson said, a silly grin on his face.

And as they shared a hearty breakfast and took warm showers, the Johnsons couldn't help but feel a newfound appreciation for the simple comforts of home, and the occasional power outage that reminded them just how much they truly had to be grateful for.

AT ZERO

From the ashes of the past, we rise anew,
In the realm of possibility, we change the view,
With nothing but hope and dreams to guide our way,
We'll forge ahead from zero, we start today.
No longer bound by chains of history,
The slate is clean, a new story to be,
We'll write our tale with passion and zeal,
For every ending holds the seed of a new reveal.
The road ahead is long and fraught with strife,
Yet we'll press on, steadfast through the night,
For every struggle makes the victory sweet,
And from the ashes, we'll take flight.
So let us start at zero, new and bold,
With hearts unburdened, stories yet untold,
For in the depths of darkness, light we'll find,
And from the ashes, we'll leave our mark behind.

MURPHY & CLEO

Once upon a time, in a cozy little house by the park, there lived a dog named Murphy and a cat named Cleo. From the minute they laid eyes on each other, it was clear that these two were not destined to be the best of friends.

Murphy was a burly bulldog, quite a character, but with a good heart, who loved nothing more than chasing after squirrels and barking at the mailman. Cleo, a sleek Siamese with a devilish grin, spent her days lounging on the windowsill, watching the birds, and plotting her next mischievous escapade.

Their human owner, Sarah, had adopted Cleo only a month ago, hoping that the two would eventually learn to get along, but as the days turned into weeks, it seemed that their rivalry was only growing stronger. One day, as Sarah sat down to enjoy her afternoon tea, she couldn't help but overhear a strange conversation between Murphy and Cleo.

"Look, Cleo, I know we haven't exactly been buddies, but we're living here together. We might as well try to make the best of it."

Yawning, Cleo replied, "Oh, Murphy, you naive silly canine. Do you really think we can just magically put aside our differences and frolic through the tulips like some cheesy pet store commercial?"

Murphy, scratching his ear, said, "Well, I don't know about frolicking, but we could at least stop trying to make each other's lives miserable. I mean, I'm tired of finding your fur in my food, and I'm sure you're tired of me snapping at you every time you try to sneak up on me."

"Hmm...you make a valid point, Murphy boy. But what about our fundamental differences? I mean, you're a dog, and I'm a cat. We're practically from different planets!"

"Look, Cleo, I know we have our differences," Murphy said, licking his paw. "But we also have a lot in common. We both love Sarah, right? And we both enjoy a good uninterrupted nap. Let's face it, we both can't stand that annoying little Yorkie yapper next door."

"You're right. That dog next door is wound waaaaaay too tight. Just about the time I close my eyes for a nap, he starts yapping incessantly. Maybe we can put aside our differences and focus on our shared dislike for that little monster."

So, Murphy and Cleo agreed to call a truce, putting aside their rivalry for the greater good of tormenting the little dog next door. While they may never be the best of friends, they learned that sometimes, you just have to find common ground, even if it's in the form of a shared nemesis.

As for Sarah, she couldn't have been happier to see her furry friends finally getting along. And while she never quite figured out why the little dog next door seemed to be avoiding their house, she was just grateful that her pets had finally found a way to coexist peacefully.

And so, Murphy and Cleo continued to live in their cozy little house by the park, occasionally sniping at each other, but always united in their quest to make the little dog next door's life a little bit more challenging. And in the end, they discovered that sometimes the best friendships are forged in the fires of rivalry and a shared desire to protect their domain.

THE DANCE OF TRUTH

Ivy loved to dance and would go to the local Elks Lodge every Wednesday and Friday nights. The music was always delightful and she was never shy about asking someone to dance.

One Friday night, the lights dimmed on the dance floor as the band began to play one of her favorite songs, *Dance Me to the End of Love*. That's when two strangers found themselves swaying to the rhythm. He was a tall, brooding man named Gerard, with eyes that seemed to hold a world of secrets, and Ivy, a graceful woman with a mysterious smile that hinted at untold stories. As their bodies moved in harmony, they found themselves drawn into a conversation that would change their lives forever.

Ivy whispered, "You know, I've seen you around town, but we've never really spoken before."

Smiling faintly, he admitted, " Yes, I've noticed you too. It's a small town, after all. I suppose it was only a matter of time before our paths crossed."

She leaned closer. "I've heard some things about you. They say you're a man with a past, a man with secrets. Is that true?"

"Secrets? Well, I suppose everyone has their secrets. But I'm not one to hide from the truth. If you want to know about my past, all you have to do is ask."

Inhaling deeply, she asked, "Alright, then. What is it that you're running from, that you've come to our little town to hide?"

Looking directly into her eyes, he said, "I suppose it's time I told someone the truth. You see, I used to be part of a powerful and dangerous organization. They taught me things – things I wish I could forget. But I realized that I couldn't live with the guilt if I performed the duties they wanted me to, so I left. I came here to start a new life, to leave all that behind."

"Why do I get the feeling that you're a man on the run? Are the authorities looking for you?"

"Oh, no, nothing like that. If you'll let me, I'd like to see you again after tonight and tell you what happened. For some reason that I haven't identified yet, I feel like I can trust you."

Ivy thought it would be best not to pursue his comment yet. Instead, she told him, "That must have been difficult, leaving everything behind. But I'm glad you did. It takes a lot of courage to face your past and try to change your future. You deserve a chance to start over."

Gazing into her eyes, "Thank you. I've been looking for someone who could understand, someone who wouldn't judge me for my past. And I think maybe I've found that person in you."

"We'll see, won't we?" she winked. "I want to take this slow, and get to know each other, aside from this dance floor."

Ivy and Gerard danced the night away, talking and laughing like two old friends. When the music was over for the evening, they walked hand in hand, their futures filled with hope. For in that slow dance, they had discovered a mystery to unravel with the power of truth, the healing balm of understanding, and even the possibility of new love.

RAPID FIRE QUANTUM LEAP

17-year old Sebastian, unlike his circle of friends, had always been fascinated by the unknown and unexplained. They often laughed at him for his beliefs and unusual interests, making him feel like an outcast.

However, one day, while browsing through his grandfather's old steamer trunk in the basement, he discovered a dusty, leather-bound journal titled "Quantum Physics and the Multiverse." Sebastian's grandfather was from Romania and never emigrated to America, so he never knew him, but had heard stories that he was an "unusual" man, keeping to himself, and misunderstood by many.

As he investigated the contents of the book, Sebastian became engrossed in the complex theories of alternate dimensions and quantum physics. The more he read, the more he realized he had stumbled upon something extraordinary. He was determined to put these theories to the test and find a way to escape his mundane life.

Over the next few months, he immersed himself in the world of quantum physics, spending countless hours studying the journal, conducting experiments, and meticulously documenting his findings. As his knowledge grew, so did his determination to prove his peers wrong and finally be accepted.

One evening, Sebastian discovered a formula that could potentially generate a quantum rift, a portal, allowing him to travel to another dimension. His excitement was through the roof, so he spent the entire night working on a prototype device, pouring all of his knowledge and passion into its creation. He found it difficult to sleep that night, but as the first rays of sunlight broke through his window, he gazed upon his masterpiece – a small, metallic device that 'hummed' with an otherworldly energy. It was a strange, foreign sound that he'd never heard before.

With a mixture of excitement and anxiety, he held his breath and activated the device. A brilliant flash of light filled the room, and a gap in the fabric of reality appeared before him. His inner voice told him he had to move forward, so without hesitation, he stepped through the portal and found himself in a parallel universe – a world vastly different from his own.

In this new dimension, Sebastian discovered a society that celebrated individuality and embraced the unknown. He was welcomed with open arms, and for the first time in his life, he felt like he truly belonged. As he explored this new world, he realized that he had found a place where he could thrive and be appreciated for his unique qualities.

Upon his return, he realized that his journey to this new dimension not only allowed him to escape the ridicule of his life, but also taught him the power of perseverance and the importance of simply being who he is, whether accepted by this world or not.

HER STUBBORN HEART

Carla had always lived a life of purpose. She was a dedicated teacher, a loving mother, and a devoted wife. However, as she approached her 60's, she began to feel the wear and tear of life taking its toll on her body. Little did she know that one summer day, her life would change forever, and her purpose would take on a whole new meaning.

It was a typical Monday morning when Carla was suddenly gripped by a crushing pain between her shoulder blades. She collapsed on the floor, sweating profusely, and unable to catch her breath. Her husband, fearing the worst, immediately called for an ambulance. As the paramedics arrived and loaded her onto the stretcher, Carla closed her eyes and surrendered to whatever fate had in store for her.

"If this is the end," she thought, "I'm OK with it."

However, fate had other plans for Carla. She was rushed to the hospital, where the emergency room doctors discovered that she had suffered a massive heart attack. The medical team worked tirelessly to stabilize her condition, and after a long and grueling surgery, Carla's life was saved.

As she lay in the hospital bed, recovering from her ordeal, Carla began to reflect on her life. She realized that despite her many accomplishments, she had never truly lived for herself.

She had always been driven by the expectations of others, and her own needs had often been set aside.

In that moment, Carla made a decision that would change the course of her life. She decided that she would no longer live for others but would, instead, focus on fulfilling her own dreams and desires. She was still here for a reason, and that reason was to live life on her own terms.

After being discharged from the hospital, Carla returned home with a newfound determination. She began to pursue her long-forgotten passion for painting, something she had always loved but had never made the time for. As she pursued her artwork, Carla discovered a sense of fulfillment and purpose she had never known.

Word of her incredible recovery and newfound passion for art began to spread throughout her community. Friends, family, and even former students reached out to offer their support and encouragement. Carla's story inspired others to reevaluate their own lives and to pursue their dreams, no matter their age or circumstances.

Years passed, and Carla's artwork continued to flourish. She held exhibitions, won awards, and even opened her own art studio. Her heart had not only survived the attack, but had also led her to discover a whole new world of creativity and purpose.

Carla's story served as a powerful reminder for others that it's never too late to chase one's dreams and that even in the face of adversity, there's always a reason to keep fighting. Her stubborn heart saved her life in more ways than one.

FELIX & HARVEY

In the heart of the high desert, a spirited coyote named Felix and a nimble jack rabbit named Harvey had been friends for years. While scampering around the desert floor one day, they stumbled upon a group of rowdy animals who decided to goad them into a race. Confident in their abilities, Felix and Harvey agreed to the challenge.

As the race began, Felix dashed ahead with great speed, confident that he would easily outrun Harvey. Meanwhile, Harvey, determined to keep up, picked up his pace and attempted to take a shortcut, leaping over a massive prickly pear cactus in his path. However, he misjudged the distance and tumbled right on top of it, needles embedded in his entire backside.

Felix, not seeing Harvey in pursuit, doubled back to find his friend battered, unable to move, whimpering in pain. Overcome with concern, Felix quickly assessed the situation and realized that he had to act fast to rescue his friend.

"Harvey, my friend. It looks like your leg is broken, too, but don't worry. I'm going to get you back to safety." All the little rabbit could do was nod his weary head.

With great care, Felix gently wiggled underneath Harvey's body and managed to hoist him onto his back, supporting his injured leg as best as he could, trying to avoid the prickly needles. He knew that getting him back to safety was his top priority, even if it meant abandoning the race.

As Felix carried Henry through the desert, he encountered several challenges, including navigating treacherous terrain and a menacing rattlesnake. However, his determination to save his friend never wavered. With each obstacle they faced, Felix's bond with his little friend grew stronger, and he realized that the race had become insignificant in comparison to the importance of Harvey's safety and their friendship.

Finally, after a long and difficult journey, Felix and Harvey reached home. With the help of their friend, the hawk, who plucked out each needle with this beak, they were able to nurse Harvey back to health. The two companions resumed their adventures together, stronger and more united than ever before.

The race that had once seemed so important had taught these two a valuable lesson about the true meaning of friendship, loyalty, and perseverance. They both realized that their bond was far more significant and enduring than any competition. And as evening began to settle on the high desert, the coyote and the jack rabbit shared a quiet moment of gratitude, knowing that they had each other's backs, no matter what challenges life might bring.

GROW UP, SAMANTHA

Samantha had always been known for her incredible sense of humor. Her friends loved her ability to lighten up any mood and make them laugh. Her jokes often had the whole room in stitches.

But one day, at a birthday party for her friend, Josh, Samantha's jokes took a dark turn and her friends began to question whether her humor had gone too far. As they gathered around the table for cake, Samantha noticed that Josh was wearing a particularly loud and unflattering shirt. Unable to resist the opportunity, she asked, "Hey, Josh, did you borrow that shirt from your grandma's closet?"

Everyone at the table laughed, and Josh, while slightly embarrassed, took the joke in stride. However, Samantha couldn't help but push the envelope. "No, seriously, Josh, where did you find that shirt? It's like it was made in the '80s and time-traveled to today!"

The laughter continued, but their friends began to feel uneasy. They could see that poor Josh was starting to feel uncomfortable, and yet, Samantha seemed oblivious to his distress.

As the night wore on, Samantha continued to make jokes about his shirt, each one more cutting than the last. Her friends tried to steer the conversation in a different direction, but Samantha was relentless.

Finally, Josh couldn't take it anymore. He thought about taking her aside to say what he needed to, but instead, mustered the courage to say it in front of everybody. "Look, Samantha, I know you're just trying to be funny in your usual way, but you're crossing a line now," he said, his voice shaking with emotion. "I don't appreciate you making fun of me like this."

Samantha, taken aback by Josh's reaction, was embarrassed and tried to play it off as harmless. "Oh, come on, buddy, it's just a shirt! I was only kidding!"

But her friends could see the hurt in Josh's eyes, and they knew that Samantha's joke had gone too far. They confronted her, telling her that her humor was bordering on bizarre and urged her to apologize to him. Her best friend, Jamie, even told her, "Damn, Sam! Grow up and act your age, not your shoe size."

At first, Samantha was defensive, insisting that she hadn't meant any harm. But as her friends explained how her words had affected their friend, she began to realize the impact of her actions. With a heavy heart, she approached Josh and apologized for her behavior.

"I'm sorry, Josh," she said, tears welling up in her eyes. "I never meant to hurt you. I just thought I was being funny, but I see now that I went too far. Can you forgive me?"

Although still hurt, Josh accepted Samantha's apology, and the two friends hugged it out. From that day forward, Samantha made a conscious effort to be more mindful of her jokes and to never let her humor come at the expense of someone else's feelings.

MAYBE IN ANOTHER LIFE

On a sweltering day in New York City, two strangers, Hallie and Stewart, found themselves standing side by side in a crowded subway station, waiting for their respective trains. As they stood there, a sense of deja vu washed over them, as if they had been in this exact situation before.

The moment their eyes met, they both felt a strange connection, a spark that seemed to transcend the boundaries of time and space. Unable to resist the urge, they struck up a conversation, discussing everything from the hot weather to their favorite books.

As their conversation continued, they discovered that they had an uncanny number of things in common. They both loved the same obscure poetry, shared a passion for travel, and even had the same favorite color. It was as if they were two halves of a whole, destined to meet in this chaotic city of millions.

However, fate had other plans for them. As their trains approached, they knew that their time together was coming to an end. With a heavy heart, Hallie turned to Stewart and said, "It's like we were meant to meet. Maybe in another life we would have been more than just strangers."

Stewart, feeling the same bittersweet sentiment, smiled sadly and replied, Yea, maybe in another life we would have been the best of friends, or even more. But for now, let's remember this moment and the connection we've shared."

As their trains pulled into the station, they exchanged a final, lingering glance, knowing that their lives would never be the same. They boarded their respective trains, their hearts filled with a mixture of longing and gratitude for the brief but meaningful encounter.

Years passed. Hallie and Stewart went on to live their lives, pursuing their dreams and forging new connections. Yet, they never forgot that hot summer day in the subway station, when they had experienced a fleeting moment of magic, a glimpse into a life that could have been. On occasion, they would both think of each other at the exact same time and smile.

They realized that their encounter had been a precious gift, a reminder that even in the most unexpected of places, there was always the possibility of finding a connection that transcended time and circumstance. And maybe, just maybe, in another life, their paths would cross again, and they would have the chance to explore the depths of their unspoken bond.

THE THIEF OF JOY

Eve and Cindy were best friends. They had known each other since they were in their early teens and shared countless memories. However, as they grew older, their bond began to weaken due to the pervasive influence of social media.

Eve, a bright and ambitious woman, had always been passionate about her career. She was a successful life coach, but her achievements seemed to pale in comparison to the seemingly prosperous lives of her social media connections. She would often find herself scrolling through their posts, feeling a sense of inadequacy and envy that she couldn't shake off.

Cindy, on the other hand, was a talented Indie artist, specializing in alcohol ink paintings, whose creations brought her immense joy. However, she, too, fell victim to the trap of social media comparison. She would frequently browse through the works of other artists, seeing all the 'likes' and comments, feeling a sense of inferiority and questioning her own abilities.

Getting together often for coffee, the two friends sat in their favorite bistro, having a heart-to-heart conversation about the adverse effects of social media on their lives.

As they sat together, Eve sighed deeply and began, "Cindy, I feel like I need to talk to you about something that's been bothering me for a while now."

Cindy, sensing her friend's unease, replied, "Of course, my friend. You know you can always talk to me about anything."

Eve hesitated for a moment before admitting, "I've been feeling really down lately, comparing myself to everyone on social media. It's like I can't help but feel like I'm not good enough, that my life isn't as exciting or successful as theirs."

Cindy nodded, her eyes revealing understanding. "I know exactly how you feel. I've been struggling with the same thing. I'll be scrolling through Instagram, looking at other artists' work, and suddenly feel like everything I've created just isn't good enough. It's like there's this constant pressure to measure up. I'll be honest, I'm feeling some self-doubt right now about what I do."

As they spoke, they realized that comparison was indeed the thief of joy. They acknowledged that social media had warped their perceptions of happiness and success, leading them to believe that their lives were somehow lacking in excitement and achievement.

Eve had an idea, "What do you say we make a pact? Let's limit our time on social media and focus on celebrating our own accomplishments. We both have a lot of passion for what we do and get joy from it. Let's make it a point to remind each other of our worth whenever the toxic influence of comparison starts to creep in again. Deal?"

Cindy was overjoyed with the pact and agreed. Over time, their friendship grew stronger than ever, as they supported and uplifted each other in their respective pursuits. They learned to find happiness in the present, rather than seeking validation from the distorted realities portrayed on social media.

MESSAGE ON THE WIND

The small suburban park was a place where children played, dogs chased tennis balls, and adults found comfort in the stillness of nature. One particularly windy day, a crumpled piece of paper tumbled across the park, caught in the gusting breeze.

The paper, once crisp and white, now bore the marks of its journey. Its edges were frayed, and its surface stained with the remnants of a life lived. As it soared through the air, it seemed to carry with it a story, a message waiting to be discovered.

Across the park, a young woman named Virginia was playing with her dog, Max. She noticed the crumpled paper as it danced through the air, and her curiosity was piqued. As the paper landed at her feet, she picked it up, her fingers brushing against the weathered parchment.

Unfolding the paper, Virginia found a message written in elegant, looping script. It read:

My dearest love,
The years have passed like the wind, but my love for you remains
steadfast, unwavering. I long for the day when we will be
reunited, our hearts entwined once more. Until then, know that I
carry your tender love with me always,
holding you close to my heart.
Yours eternally,

A.

Virginia's jaw dropped as she read the heartfelt message, a sense of wonder and mystery filling her. She wondered where the paper had come from and who had written such a beautiful letter. Her imagination ran wild, conjuring up images of a lost love and a longing that transcended time and distance.

Determined to solve the mystery, she took the crumpled paper home, her mind racing with questions and possibilities. That night, she shared the story with her family, who were equally captivated by the unexpected message and its unknown origins.

She asked her mom if she'd help her find out more about it. Together, they took on the task of unraveling the mystery of the crumpled paper and the love story it held within its creases. As they delved deeper, they discovered that the message was written by a man named Alexander, who had lost his true love, Dierdre, many years ago.

Alexander had carried the paper with him, a tangible reminder of his undying love for her. One fateful day, as he stood on a hill overlooking the park, the wind had snatched the crumpled paper from his grasp, carrying it away on its journey.

As the story of Alexander and Dierdre's love spread throughout the community, the park became a symbol of hope and the enduring power of love. And though the mystery of the crumpled paper was never completely solved, its message of love and longing lived on, carried by the wind and etched into the hearts of all who heard its tale.

LIFE'S ENIGMA

The meaning of life, a riddle profound,
    A quest for truth, often unbound.
    Through joy and pain, we each must find,
    Our purpose in this world so unkind.
    We strive and toil, with hearts so pure,
    To seek the truth, to feel secure.
    In every breath, in every sigh,
    We search for answers to justify.
    Yet, in the chaos, in the strife,
    A single truth, a simple life.
    To love, to live, to learn, to grow,
    That's all there is, high or low.
    So, let us cherish each fleeting day,
    For life's true meaning lies in the way
    We live, we love, and face the end,
    With courage and hope, the perfect blend.

DISCOVERY AT THE BEACH

In the quaint coastal town of Sea Lodge, there lived a family of three: a father, mother, their 10 year old daughter, Pam, and their loyal family dog, a yellow lab named Checkers. The family loved spending their weekends at the beach, enjoying the sun, sand, and surf, with Checkers never missing a chance to bop in and out of the waves. The beach was his second home.

One Saturday morning, the family set out for their favorite spot called Agate Beach, with Checkers leading the way, his tail wagging excitedly. With no clouds or fog, the sun was unusually bright, casting golden hues across the shoreline, as the family settled in for a day of relaxation and fun. Pam's mom kept slathering sunscreen on her daughter's fair, freckled skin, hoping to avoid the pain of a sunburn later.

"Mom, can you put some extra goop on my nose? It's already feeling pretty hot!" Pam exclaimed. Her mom put another layer on her nose and then she ran off to catch up to Checkers.

As the afternoon wore on, Pam and Checkers became restless, eager to explore the beach and its many wonders. Each time they came here, they discovered something they hadn't before. They ventured down the shoreline, their eyes scanning the sand for special pieces of driftwood and maybe some sand crabs. It wasn't long before they came across a small, mysterious hole in the sand, just as the tide began to go out.

Curiosity getting the best of them, Pam approached the hole cautiously, her heart racing with excitement. "Ooooh, a new discovery," she thought. Checkers came alongside to see what she was looking at. As they got closer, they noticed a peculiar, elongated shell protruding from the sand. Intrigued, Pam reached out to touch it, only to watch in amazement as it quickly retreated back into the hole. Checkers got scared and jumped back, his nose twitching to catch a scent of whatever it was, but keeping a close eye on Pam. She looked at him and said, "What the heck was *that*?"

Determined to uncover this mysterious treasure, Pam started to dig, her excitement growing with each scoop of sand. All of a sudden, Checkers came closer and began digging, too. His paws were going so fast, she had to slow him down. Pam was afraid they would uncover something dangerous and she didn't want whatever it was to hurt him. She kept digging cautiously and as the hole deepened, they finally uncovered a large, beautiful clam, nestled in the cool, damp sand.

Excited by their discovery, Pam called out to her parents, "Mom, Dad, come check out what Checkers and I found!" They rushed over to see what all the excitement was about. Dad said, "Wow! That's a razor clam. They're also called filter feeders because they have siphons to draw in water and then extract nutrients from their environment. See how its shell looks like a straight razor? That's how they got their name. Good find, Pam!"

"How do you know all that, Dad?"

"Well, honey, I learned about all kinds of shellfish when I was going to college in Seattle. None of us guys had much money, so we often went fishing, dug for clams, and did some crabbing. Razor clams are pretty tasty if you can catch 'em," he laughed.

The family was delighted by the razor clam, marveling at its unique appearance and how they discovered it. As the sun began to set, Dad built a bonfire and the family gathered around, chatting about their newfound treasure, snapping pictures and recalling stories of their past beach adventures. With Checkers resting happily by their side, the family relaxed in the magic of the moment, knowing that their treasured discovery would forever hold a special memory.

On the way home, their hearts were filled with gratitude for each other and a newfound appreciation for the simple joys of life. They had learned that sometimes the most extraordinary treasures can be found in the most unexpected places, waiting to be discovered by those with curious minds.

I'M SORRY, MY LOVE

Morris always thought that providing well for his family was enough. He worked hard, paid the bills, and ensured his wife, Victoria, had security and comfort. He loved her deeply, but he never quite grasped the importance of the little things.

Victoria loved flowers; their vibrant colors, their fragrances, and she especially loved to wear them in her hair. She would often mention how beautiful a bouquet looked in a shop window or how lovely a single rose could be, but Morris dismissed it as a frivolous desire.

One day, as they walked past a florist, Victoria pointed at a beautiful bunch of lilies and said, "Aren't they beautiful, honey? They remind me of the ones we had at our wedding." Morris looked at the flowers and shrugged, "I suppose they are, but I've got so many things on my mind right now, dear."

Over the years, Victoria would drop subtle hints about her love for flowers, but John would only buy them for her on special occasions, and even then, only after she had dropped the hint.

As the years passed, their love grew stronger, but the unfulfilled desire for her husband to give her flowers remained. She never complained, though. She was happy with what she had and loved him deeply.

After 35 years of marriage, Victoria suddenly passed away from pneumonia. As Morris laid a perfectly arranged bunch of white lilies on her casket, he couldn't help but feel the pain of remorse. He remembered all the times he had dismissed her love for flowers, thinking his role as the breadwinner was enough.

In that moment, he wished he had understood the importance of those little things earlier. He wished he had showered her with flowers while she was alive, not just because she loved them, but because they were a symbol of their love, a testament to the life they had shared together.

He whispered to her, "I'm sorry, my love. Please forgive me. I never realized how much they meant to you. I wish I had paid more attention."

As he stood there, tears streaming down his cheeks, he made a promise to himself. He would never forget the lesson Victoria had inadvertently taught him – the importance of the little things in life.

ABOUT THE AUTHOR

"I write to be a source of inspiration to others, potentially sparking new,
creative ideas for my readers." ~ Regina Arnold

Regina Arnold lives and writes in the Willamette Valley of Oregon and is the author of *Bye for Now, P.J. - How Writing Letters to My Departed Son Moved Me from Broken to Better,*

and *Sunrise After Rain - Healing, Hope and Strength for Grieving Mothers.*

Her creative spirit extends into both fiction and nonfiction, enriching the lives of her readers. When she doesn't have her hands on the keyboard, Regina explores the beauty of Oregon, capturing valuable moments with her camera, enjoying connections with the canine world, and embracing new adventures with friends.

www.ingramcontent.com/pod-product-compliance
Lightning Source LLC
Chambersburg PA
CBHW022004120726

47992CB00001B/411